THREAT LEVEL: HELLFIRE

FBI MAGICAL THREATS DIVISION™
BOOK TWO

TR CAMERON   MARTHA CARR   MICHAEL ANDERLE

DON'T MISS OUR NEW RELEASES

Join the LMBPN email list to be notified of new releases
and special promotions (which happen often) by following
this link:

http://lmbpn.com/email/

THE THREAT LEVEL: HELLFIRE TEAM

Thanks to our JIT Readers:

Dave Hicks
Dorothy Lloyd
Christopher Gilliard
Zacc Pelter
Peter Manis
Diane L. Smith
Jan Hunnicutt

Editor
SkyFyre Editing Team

For those who seek wonder around every corner and in each turning page. Thank you choosing to share the adventure with me. And, as always, for Dylan and Laurel.

— TR Cameron

At seven o'clock Monday morning, Billie Keller walked into work at the FBI's Criminal, Cyber, International, Magical, Response, and Services Branch headquarters. She waved at the security guard behind the semicircular desk in the lobby and headed for the elevator that would take her two levels down to the home of her division, Magical Threats. She was the first leader of the newly formed unit and was well aware of both the honor and expectations of her new job.

As she exited the elevator, she nodded as she always did at the FBI logo positioned on the entryway floor, then took the left-hand door to head into her domain. It felt vaguely like bowing before entering a dojo, something she had done countless times. Before she made it halfway down the long corridor toward her office, someone with a female voice called from behind, "Hey, boss."

Billie backpedaled and peered in through the now open office door of the team's infomancer, Izzy Sato. Izzy wore a vintage black dress that looked more appropriate for Halloween than the office, but it complemented the asymmetric black hair that hid half her face. The infomancer had straightened in her chair to look at Billie through the gap between her lower and upper rows of monitors.

Billie frowned. "How did you open the door from there?"

Izzy laughed and waggled her fingers. "Magic."

"No, really." Izzy's magic worked mainly in the simulated reality of the magical dark web, although she doubtless had the basic skills most magicals possessed, which would be sufficient to open the door.

The other woman smiled. "Cleverly concealed actuators and a remote control."

"Ah. You almost had me there," Billie lied. "You're here early."

"I'm still here from yesterday. Slept over."

A part of Billie's mind observed that the other woman looked more put-together after an all-nighter than she did after a good night's sleep. She mentally informed the annoying part that it could keep its opinions to itself. She wasn't nearly as impressive-looking as the infomancer, but her blonde hair was well-cut and styled, her business suit looked sharp, and no one ever covered their child's eyes when she passed them on the street or anything. Out loud, she asked, "You're aware you're not required to work weekends, right?"

"An infomancer's work is never done."

Billie walked into the room and around to stand behind the desk with Izzy. "So, why the long night?"

The other woman tilted her head to look at her. "Something was chewing on me. I had some systems working on it and wanted to stay close."

"And?"

"I think I found Colm Raffertey's base of operations."

Excitement thrilled through Billie. Colm Raffertey was the leader of the gang that had broken into the National Geographic Museum. He had fled when the heist got out of hand and had left her, her team, and the Critical Incident Response unit fighting a creature the news outlets were calling the Crystal Colossus. His continued freedom had been a constant sore at the back of her mind.

"Hang on." She called her second-in-command, Caleb Armstrong. "Report to Izzy's office."

He arrived a moment later. "What's up?" As usual, he had foregone a tie but wore a crisp white button-down under a sports coat. His clipped brown hair always made him look like he'd come out of basic training or something, an impression his athletic build supported.

Billie replied, "I have to go to the division heads' meeting. You two work this. I'll be back as soon as I can."

When she returned two hours later, Caleb was still there. He looked up. "How does it feel to be the only one without an administrative assistant?"

Billie scowled. "Shut up, or I'll promote you to the job."

He laughed. "Dictator move. You're really letting this leadership thing go to your head."

Izzy countered, "I like it. You'd make a great admin, Caleb. We could dress you in, like, a vest with no shirt. Eye candy for meetings."

He stuck his tongue out at the infomancer, who returned the gesture.

Billie sat on the couch set perpendicular to Izzy's workstation. "What do you have?"

Izzy swiveled her chair to face her, and Caleb leaned back out of the way. "I was running facial recognition during the thing at the museum. I didn't get any matches then, but I had an agent looking for matches just in case. This person showed up on some local cameras over the weekend." Izzy gestured at her monitor, where four grainy images showed what might have been the same man.

Billie observed, "He could be anyone."

The other woman nodded and brushed her hanging hair behind her ear. It escaped an instant later and went back over her face. "Yes, but my systems say it was him at the museum. So, I sent a worm in to look for him."

"Into what, exactly?"

Izzy looked sheepish. "Uh, DCPD's camera system."

Billie lifted an eyebrow. "With permission?"

"Not really."

The revelation wasn't a shock. It was more or less standard infomancer behavior, as Billie understood it. "Will they be able to trace you back?"

Izzy snorted. "Hardly."

"All right. Where is he?"

Izzy tapped some buttons, and the screen changed. "Here."

To Billie, it appeared to be a generic section of the city shown from above. As a newcomer, she didn't know the neighborhoods nearly as well as she knew the terrain in

Las Vegas, where she'd worked previously. "Doesn't look like anything special."

"What if I do this?" An overlay of the city's subway system, a familiar image to anyone in DC, appeared atop the current image. Beneath the building Izzy had indicated was a small striped section. "What is that?"

"An abandoned portion of the subway, apparently." The infomancer sounded satisfied.

Billie leaned forward. "All right, now I'm interested. What's down there?"

"No way to tell. But nearby cameras show that this building has a lot of people going in and not coming out for a long time afterward, if at all. Of course, it could be magic on the other side taking them anywhere. Portals are so inconvenient when you're trying to do surveillance."

Billie looked at Caleb. "You think there's something there?"

His expression answered before his voice did. "I do."

"Me too. Let's get some enhanced surveillance going on the location. Send Anya to place some cameras, use whoever you need."

With a grin, Caleb asked, "What will you be doing?"

Billie rolled her eyes. "Completing paperwork and reviewing admin resumes."

He laughed. "I'll stay here and help Izzy."

"Thanks, buddy."

"Don't mention it."

That evening, the whole team gathered in the conference room to watch the cameras Anya, the team's scout, had placed. Onyx, the representative of the pixie council who had attached herself to Billie, ostensibly to watch over her, was present as well. Her spiky electric blue hair made her impossible to miss, but if it hadn't, the black pants, crop top, and crisscrossing studded belts would have set her apart.

The chat was casual and friendly, but with an edge of anticipation. When a big SUV pulled up and Colm Raffertey climbed out of it, everyone in the room sat up straighter.

Izzy reported, "Confirmation from my system. That's Raffertey."

Billie snapped, "All right, people. Let's do it." As they headed for the staircase that would take them to their arming room one level up, Billie sent a message to the head of the Critical Incident Response division, Brandon Shale. With both of their divisions in the same branch, it was natural for them to back one another up when needed. Izzy's research had identified a spot where the abandoned spur was to connect to the functioning lines, and CIR would watch over that to prevent Raffertey or his people from escaping in that direction.

Everyone moved quickly to their lockers when they reached the equipment room. The sense of energy from her team was palpable as they pulled on body armor and associated equipment. Izzy's voice in their earpieces announced every few minutes that nothing had changed.

As soon as each person was properly armored, they headed into the next room for weapons selection. Billie took her usual rifle and pistol while Caleb selected a shotgun and a pistol. The rest chose rifles, although Quentin would have doubtless preferred his sniper rifle.

Unfortunately for him, this particular mission wasn't a match for that tactic.

Deacon, the team's infiltration expert, teased, "Don't worry, big guy. One of these days you'll get to use the big gun again."

Billie laughed. "Too bad you weren't there when the giant crab attacked the DC waterfront."

Onyx chuckled beside her. That had been Billie's first adventure in DC, some time before she'd been selected to head up the Magical Threats division. It was also where she had met the pixie for the first time. She'd never expected to see her again and had been pleasantly surprised when the pixie council had sent Onyx to watch her.

When they were all fully geared, Billie looked them over even though they had all already checked on one another's equipment. She nodded. "We're ready, Anya."

The team's scout opened a portal to a spot a block away from and out of the line of sight of the building. Billie cast a veil around everything after she was through. When everyone was on the proper side and the rift was closed, she asked, "Anything to worry about, Izzy?"

"Neither the cameras nor the drone show activity anywhere on the block."

Billie ordered, "Shadow, go."

She sensed Anya's departure but didn't see it since the woman had cast her own veil as she moved away. The camera showed a slight wobble in the air near the front door but gave no other indication of her scout's presence. A moment later, an image from the camera Anya had strung through the tiny hole she'd drilled in the door showed an empty room.

Izzy instructed, "Hold one." A moment later, she confirmed, "Alarm deactivated. You're good to go."

Ten seconds after that, Anya advised, "Lock's open."

Billie didn't put into words the admiration she felt for her team's professionalism. There would be time for that later. Instead, she ordered, "All right, everyone, keep it frosty. Let's move."

CHAPTER TWO

nya had already pushed the door open by the time Billie arrived but hadn't crossed the threshold. Billie asked, "Traps?"

The scout nodded. "Tripwire in front of us, cleverly set a little farther ahead than you'd expect it, and only a centimeter or two above the floor. I'm guessing others are present, but I haven't spotted them yet."

"Internal cameras?"

Izzy replied, "No wireless ones that I can detect. I can't speak to a wired system. They don't have a network I can find, only the dedicated controls for the security alarm on the door."

"Then we'll go slow. Anya leads, I'm second. Switching my view to thermal." Billie did so, but the additional visual mode offered no useful information.

Anya marked the tripwire and guided everyone past it. When everyone was inside, she closed the door again and locked it, then added a small virtual tag that would appear on their displays to remind them of the trap.

Billie turned in a slow circle with her rifle braced at her shoulder as it had been since she stepped inside. No targets presented themselves. A dilapidated bar ran along the far wall, its nicks, scratches, and long gouges indicating the room had seen many drunken inhabitants and probably fairly regular brawls. More than one heart was visible on its top, and several had large Xs slashed through them.

Izzy informed them, "This used to be a lodge. Private club. Several different groups held it during the years, but no one relevant to Raffertey. I can't find any records of recent sales, which likely means an infomancer wiped that data out."

Anya reported, "We're good, no more tripwires or other traps."

The scout had searched the room while the team stayed where she'd put them. Now they fanned out to search.

Deacon observed, "Lots of evidence of foot traffic on the floor, but this doesn't read like a place they hung out for any length of time."

Quentin replied, "Agreed, Preacher. This room is for show, not for use."

The room held several doors. Most led to innocuous places, like a pair of bathrooms, a storage room, and what had probably been the place where beer kegs had been held long ago. One was locked, however, and behind it was another door, made of metal and offering no visible means of opening it.

Billie magnified her vision and found the spot where the bolts met the frame in the tiny seam between door and wall. "Quentin."

The team's sniper and temporary demolitions expert

until they got someone to fill that specialty role placed two shaped charges on the seam between door and wall at Billie's direction. As he backed away, he muttered, "We need an expert for this."

Billie replied, "Yeah, yeah, no whining during missions." She spoke the command to activate the explosives. The blocks blew out the fasteners, and the door swung open to reveal a wooden staircase that led down and looked no more stable than the rest of the building's first floor.

Izzy warned, "Detecting frequencies in the stairwell that might be triggers for something nasty."

"Block them."

"That will reveal your presence."

Caleb observed, "The explosives probably did that already, Z."

Izzy announced, "Done. All blocked except ours."

Billie ordered, "Shadow leads, then me." They moved down the stairs carefully, each member of the team pointing their weapon toward the door at the bottom, which was the same kind as the one at the top.

As Quentin moved toward it to place charges, Anya warned, "Cueball, stop. That door could be electrified or something. It has a weird haze in my display."

Billie noticed it now that the other woman had mentioned it. "That would be weird, but something is going on."

"It could be anything. Maybe magic seepage, maybe a power cable with poor shielding. But I'm pretty sure we shouldn't touch the door if we can avoid it."

Billie replied, "Fortunately, we can."

Quentin held up two more shaped charges, and she

lifted her hands palms-up and allowed magic to spill from them toward the blocks. Both lifted from his palms and moved toward the door.

When they were inches away, she instructed, "Shadow, give me a force shield behind the charges with a hole so my magic can get through. Preacher, another behind hers."

Even non-aggressive magic was often hindered by magical shields. When both reported they had done so, she pressed the objects against the seam and spoke the signal to detonate them.

The door flew open, and a hail of bullets came from beyond it into the stairwell. They penetrated the shields, which meant their foes had anti-magic rounds. Everyone except Billie and Anya was too high up the staircase to be hit from the guns' positions.

She grunted as a bullet clanged off an armor plate and snapped, "Grenades, Shadow." Her hands were already moving toward hers, and together they threw four into the room beyond, then reflexively slapped up force shields so they couldn't be kicked back out.

They detonated in pairs separated by only a second. Anya, Billie, and the rest of her team charged through the entrance with Onyx right behind Billie, as usual. Billie drew her pistol as she ran in and used the other hand to hurl a wave of force at the room's occupants. A magical shield intercepted the attack before it could connect, but that shield hadn't been able to mitigate the combined concussive force of four flash-bang grenades in close proximity.

Billie located the person who was slowest to bring their gun up, figuring it had the highest probability of being the magical supplying the shield, aimed her pistol, and pulled the trigger. The anti-magic round slammed into the other woman's shoulder and sent her spinning down to the floor. Billie used bursts of force magic to knock the remaining guns up as the defenders pulled their triggers at her incoming team. Their bullets went into the ceiling.

She ran toward the nearest enemy and delivered a jumping side kick to his chest. His surprised look as he flew backward was priceless. Her boots hit the floor, and she turned toward the next to discover that Onyx had already engaged him. He was frantically trying to block with his rifle as the human-sized pixie slammed her clubs down at him like an energetic drummer on a floor tom.

He missed a block, and her club caught him on the collarbone, cracking it. Onyx's next move was to sweep his legs out with a quick twist of her body and smash of her clubs. He hit the floor, and Billie blasted her opponent and Onyx's with lightning until they quit moving. The rest of the team had handled the others with varying degrees of injury to their enemies.

Deacon observed, "Only six, surely this can't be all of them."

Caleb added, "Raffertey's not here."

Billie looked around but saw no other obvious exit from the room. "Z?"

Izzy replied, "Scanning."

Several seconds later, the outline of a door on the far wall appeared in Billie's display. Despite looking as hard as she could, she saw no seam for it. "Nice craftsmanship."

The infomancer replied, "Shadow, pull out the breaker."

Anya lifted a device from her belt and started moving it along the wall.

After half a minute, Izzy directed, "Hold there." Fifteen seconds later, the wall moved inward, then slid aside. "Magnetic code. Interesting tech. You don't see that very often."

Billie moved forward until she could see what lay beyond the door. A metal staircase that switched back on itself in a rectangular pattern descended into the depths. "That's way down. Be careful not to fall, people." Billie cast a veil over her team as they gathered, careful to enhance the sound-deadening properties given the metal, then followed Anya as the scout led the way.

Izzy quipped, "I'm sure there's nothing bad waiting for you down below."

Deacon groaned. "Way to go. Now you've cursed us. Next time, you get to lead."

Izzy laughed. "Bringing me on a mission would be bad. Letting me lead would be a guaranteed total party kill. Just, you know, be careful."

Fortunately, the conversation stopped before Billie had to stop it. Secretly, she agreed with the infomancer's sarcastic comment and was positive that trouble waited for them at the bottom.

CHAPTER THREE

Billie had expected to find traps on the stairwell, but they had spotted none despite using various visual modes and magic detection to search for them. The door at the bottom was unlocked, and they moved through it and spread out to the sides in a preplanned arrangement, hidden from sight and sound by the veil that covered them.

The cavernous space was dusty, although footprints in the dust showed evidence of recent trespasses. They stood at the end of a long, flat subway platform. To their right, a ledge led down to the disused track, and nothing suggested that power flowed to the dangerous third rail.

Another set of tracks beyond it was separated from the first by a row of pillars supporting the roof high above, and past that, space for another platform had been carved out from the stone but never finished. The tiled wall on their left held two doors that both showed signs of use.

Hidden speakers crackled into life as a man stated, "You shouldn't have come here."

Billie reached out to the nearby rubble, grabbed pieces

with her magic, and raised them in front of her team as a protective shield. With a mechanical whine, three objects she had taken for piled junk but now realized had been covered by dirty tarps rose from the floor. She snapped, "Turrets."

More debris came up to shield them as the other magicals joined in the defense. Caleb and Quentin began laying rounds from shotgun and rifle, respectively, into the nearest turret. The return fire struck the rubble, which was now making almost a solid wall except where her people were shooting. All three were down in short order with no injuries, although one bullet had gotten through the shields and caught Caleb in the armor on his chest.

He groaned. "That's gonna leave a mark."

Onyx offered, "Way to whine, whiner."

Billie ignored the pixie and ordered, "Near door. Stay out of the firing line." She gathered her magic as she walked toward it, then blasted the door off its hinges and into the room beyond. Gunfire immediately came through the opening, as did a wash of flame. She muttered, "One magical at least."

Anya asked, "Other door?"

"Negative. We'll use this one. I'll do an outer shell of force. You do an inner shell of ice." She created the protective barrier, then summoned the debris she'd used before to create a physical one in front of them. Then she pushed it through the door and charged in after it. The rubble handled the bullets well, but some of the fire snuck through. Fortunately, her shield took care of most of it, and what it didn't, Anya's ice did.

Inside, they encountered a single shooter and a lone

magical. Anya took down the magical with a blast from her rifle, and Billie slammed lightning magic into the unshielded human until he collapsed, unconscious. In the pause afterward, running footsteps were audible from the opening that led from the back of the room.

Billie snapped, "They're running. Let's go."

She led the chase with Anya one step behind on her right, and Onyx a few behind on her left. As they rounded a corner, a bullet flew in their direction, but Billie tossed the metal shard of turret she carried into the air and used her magic to intercept the bullet with it. Anya's shots took the unwise straggler down.

Another magical appeared, and Onyx selected two of the studs on her belt, converted them into dust, and threw them into the air. Billie used force magic to create a gust of wind that carried them to their foe, who had failed to close his shield fully. A moment later, coughing erupted beyond the barrier, and it fell, as did the magical, who dropped to his knees.

Billie asked, "What was it this time?"

"Essentially, ghost pepper."

She laughed. "Cruel."

The pixie countered, "Better than killing them."

Anya shrouded the fallen magical in lightning until he was unconscious, which was probably a mercy, all things considered.

The corridor ahead opened into a larger space. The team approached cautiously. Each of the magicals had items floating nearby, ready to bring up as shields against bullets.

The chamber had been drilled out but never finished.

The floor and walls were treacherously uneven bare rock. Another opening had been created on the far side, and voices came from it, followed by explosions. A wash of dust entered the room from the tunnel, and by the time Billie and the others pushed it out of the way, their enemies were in the room.

The moment held as they stared at the newcomers and were stared at in return. A dozen of his people surrounded Colm Raffertey, a mixture of magicals and not, to judge by the way they were positioning themselves for the fight to come.

Billie's allies shot first, but the opposition used their tactics against them, pulling rocks from the floors and walls and using them to deflect the incoming rounds. Billie had a moment to be impressed at how skillfully they did so, finesse rather than brute blocking the way she normally did, and filed away a mental note to consider whether she could do the same.

She ran at the nearest, keeping the barrier in front of her as she drew her sentient shape-changing dagger Dorian from his sheath. She cast blasts of electricity through it and between the pieces of her shield as she charged, hoping to catch someone unguarded, but the opposing magicals had everyone shielded. Billie reached the one closest to her team, used a flick of magic to force his gun to shoot up into the ceiling, and punched him in the chest with a force-aided fist.

Billie crouched to slash the edge of her blade along his thigh as he backpedaled. As the leg collapsed underneath him, she spun backward and delivered a heel kick to his head. Her foe flipped through the air and landed hard on his back, out of the fight.

Magic hammered into her from two sides, but the skintight shield she had around herself handled it.

Onyx barked, "Duck, Basher."

Billie dropped to the ground. The pixie jumped over her and crashed down on the next enemy in line. The man had chosen to embrace the classic wizard image, sporting a long beard and a crooked wand that was as gnarled and scarred as Onyx's clubs.

The pixie's first two blows, delivered with all of her momentum behind them, were stopped by his shield, but the knee she slammed up into his solar plexus got partially through. He coughed, his shield wavered, and she slammed him in the knee with one of the clubs. He dropped, and Onyx pulled pixie dust from her belt and blew it in his face.

Billie had spent the time it took Onyx to drop him by knocking gun barrels out of line to protect her team. Raffertey had remained in the back, apart from the fight-ing, with a single magical to defend him. She saw the desire to escape in his eyes and shifted to get between him and the exit. He awarded the move a thin, almost regretful smile.

Finally, when everyone was down except him and the magical he stood behind, she called, "All right, Raffertey. Give it up. Enough people have been hurt today."

He laughed. "I don't think so." His hand emerged from inside his jacket, and he held up the detonator switch so she could see it. The thick black cylinder had a large red button on the top that he pressed as she watched. "If I release this, boom. No one gets to go home. Now, move out of the way."

Billie shook her head. "Not going to happen." She placed tight force shields around her team, then added more on the outside. She hoped the other magicals were doing the same. If the chamber crashed down atop them, she only needed to hold the rock away for long enough for someone to make a portal, and they would be out safely.

Raffertey scowled. "Damn my brother and his stupidity for starting all this." He released the red button, cringed, and looked wildly around, but nothing happened.

Billie was as surprised as he was until Izzy's voice came out of the interface packs they wore so Raffertey could hear her.

"Maybe next time stick to wired doomsday devices, buddy. Wireless is so very susceptible to jamming."

His face paled as the magical beside him raised his arms and stepped away. Billie, Anya, and Deacon covered them both with lightning until they passed out.

Billie called Brandon Shale. "Y'all okay?"

"Yeah. They took one look at us and ran away. You get him?"

"I got him. Thanks for the help." She killed the connection and gestured toward the people on the floor. "All right, let's collect these fallen losers and get them behind bars where they belong."

CHAPTER FOUR

Billie and her team spent the next morning engaged in a detailed debrief on the events of the previous day. The result was overall satisfaction with their performance with some areas identified for potential improvement, as there always were. Afterward, they ordered lunch in for everyone, and she and Caleb took theirs to her office and went through resumes for the open administrative position. Twenty remained after the initial review round, and they went through them one by one.

After they'd reviewed them all, Caleb pointed out, "This is a tough hire. We need someone who can handle routine bookkeeping and communication but also make sure we're always stocked up on anti-magic ammunition and explosives, not to mention medical kits, potions, and coffee for your pathetic addiction."

Billie laughed. "Liking things with flavor other than dirt is not a pathetic addiction."

"Everyone who's normal would beg to differ."

"If that's being normal, I'm not interested."

Caleb lifted one of the resumes and extended it to her. As she took it, he observed, "I think this is the best one. He's more or less a jack of all trades, having worked for the Secret Service, the FBI, and in the corporate world. More an executive assistant than an administrative one, but he's available. Plus, you could call yourself an executive. I know you secretly desire to be fancy like that."

She nodded while reviewing the material on the paper. "I am fancy."

"Bring him in?"

"Definitely. Set it up for tomorrow."

The minutiae of running a division, including the requisite call to Brandon Shale to thank him again for his team's participation, filled the rest of the day. She had originally found him a little much to take, definitely possessed of "a surfeit of testosterone," as Izzy had called it, but continued exposure had engendered an honest appreciation of his skills. She invited him out to the team's happy hour that evening, and though he declined, he seemed pleased to have been remembered.

At five, Billie and her team headed out to the Hard Case and took over several tables in a corner of the main bar. Onyx joined them shortly after and claimed the seat at Billie's side, which had been left open for the pixie by unspoken agreement.

Billie considered it quite amazing how well Onyx had integrated into the team when she thought about it. Having the other woman there was now as natural as any other part of her job even though she knew that illusion disguised wings, and that the twigs secured in her overlapping belts could become clubs through the application of the pixie's magic. She wished she could carry her weapons so well hidden.

The bartenders were happy because her team was polite and tipped well, and the rest of the crowd seemed amused by their presence as they described recent events. Each shared their perspective on the adventure of the day before as a story, rather than in the analytical breakdown they'd offered earlier.

This was an important ritual that Billie had learned from her mentor when she'd been in charge of the Vegas AET. People had to celebrate wins whenever they could. Eventually, the team would lose a battle, and they would need the memory of moments like this to carry them through the pain of those experiences. Hopefully, the inevitable would hold off for a long time.

When the group started to break up, Billie decided she didn't feel like spending the evening at home. She invited Izzy, Onyx, Eileen, and Anya out to watch her friend Erin at her DJ gig. Anya declined, but the others readily accepted and broke up to prepare.

Back at home, Billie dug into her closet and found a pair of black leather pants that fit her well, boots with buckles that reached up over her calves, and a top that would reveal a little of her toned stomach if she wound up dancing aggressively. She was in the mood to dance. The thought crossed her mind that she should call Owen and invite him since she'd promised him a night out, but she discarded it immediately. She wanted relaxation, and while Owen engendered many feelings in her, relaxation wasn't one of them.

After applying some light makeup, she slid in some

hoop earrings that smacked against the side of her neck as she twisted her head this way and that, teased her hair until people would take note of it, and added one of her favorite necklaces and a few rings. A bracelet was the final touch, and she was ready to go.

Onyx was waiting for her when Billie reached the lobby of her apartment building. The pixie wore her normal outfit of boots, dark pants, and crisscrossing belts, but had put on a shimmering blue top that matched her electric hair color. She had also deepened her makeup with eye shadow and liner in dark purple that extended a good inch past the edge of her eye.

"Looking good, pixie."

Onyx grinned. "Same to you, elf."

Billie tilted her head. "Did I ever tell you I had elf in my heritage?"

"No. But it's obvious when you know what to look for, and I do. I have to say though…" Onyx tapped one of her own pointed ears. "You'd look good with these."

Billie laughed. "But then I couldn't surprise anyone with my magic the way I can now."

"Fair point. Not everyone is willing to sacrifice for beauty."

The autonomous car Billie had summoned pulled up, and they climbed in for the short ride to Club Barrage. Eileen was waiting outside in a red dress that was tight on top but flared out at her waist to swirl when she moved. She, too, was made up for an evening out and looked excited.

Izzy arrived a moment later in a shimmering blue dress that was the most modern thing Billie had ever seen the infomancer wear. She still wore the many-buckled boots, which made for an interesting mix of styles. They all went inside together.

Billie had gotten the impression from how Erin had spoken of it that Club Barrage was a fairly ritzy place, but it hid this aspect well. The only place it was visible was the accents of chrome and glass on the bars and the quality of the neon on the walls. Otherwise, it was a high-energy upscale dance club, like many she'd been in before. The left and right sides of the rectangular space were long bars filled with patrons three deep seeking libations. At the far end was the DJ stage, dominated by flashing lights and other visual distractions.

Erin stood behind it with one earpiece of a set of head-phones pressed against her ear as she reached out with the other hand and manipulated things unseen on the board in front of her. The front of the DJ booth and the wall behind her were both video screens, and music videos tied to the songs played in flashes.

Billie headed for the bar on the left, passing several security people in black trousers and button-downs who kept a careful eye on the club. She had expected an upstairs section where the coolest people hung out, but there was no such visible part of the club. The second story appeared to be dedicated to lighting and sound equipment. The pace of people going to the bars and getting drinks made Billie think that Erin probably hadn't exaggerated about the lucrative business the club did.

She and her friends headed to the dance floor with drinks in hand. Billie lost her sense of time as she danced, talked, laughed, and stayed there until she started to get tired. Eileen looked like she needed a break too, but Onyx and Izzy were still very wound up and managed to keep them dancing until Erin finished her set and vanished through a door at the back of the booth. Billie headed in that general direction and found a different door with a guard in front of it. She explained who she was, and the guard spoke into a small microphone.

A moment later he nodded. "You can go back."

The VIP section she had expected was beyond the door. The luxurious area had couches, stuffed chairs, and its own private bar with two servers moving from person to person in a constant flow of service.

Erin ran up and hugged Billie. "What did you think?" Her friend's makeup was set for the stage with glitter above her eyes and dramatic stripes on her cheeks.

"Are you really doing anything when you wave your hands around up there?"

Erin laughed. "A DJ never reveals her secrets. Who are your friends?"

Billie made the introductions, and Erin led them to a couch with several chairs nearby. They took seats, ordered drinks, and chatted. Erin fit in well with her team, Billie thought, then corrected, with her friends. Her coworkers had quickly become that, and Erin was on her way to being that as well.

Each time the door opened, everyone in the room looked up, including them. As it happened again, Erin stood, went to the man who stepped through, and hugged him. His return embrace looked professional rather than personal, and Billie figured he was a VIP, not a friend.

Erin escorted him over. "Billie, Izzy, Onyx, and Eileen, this is Derik. He's one of my favorite people here."

He chuckled. "Erin's the best, don't you think?"

While the others agreed with varying levels of enthusiasm, Billie worked at keeping her expression still. Something about him didn't feel right. His tone, the way he treated Erin, or maybe the way his smile didn't seem to reach his eyes. He was handsome enough with dark hair and expensive clothes in perfect business casual.

When it was her turn to speak, she replied, "Erin's great. What do you do? Something that pays well, based on your suit."

He chuckled, seeming pleased that she'd noticed. "I run some businesses. Boring stuff, really, but occasionally lucrative."

Erin patted his arm. "Don't let him fool you. Quite lucrative, and he does more than run them. He built them from the ground up. Derik is the epitome of the self-made man. Now, how about we get you a drink?"

As Erin drew him away, Onyx leaned toward Bille. "What is it?"

She frowned. "You weren't supposed to notice anything."

The pixie waved it off. "I'm sure no one else did. What is it?" The other two were looking at her now, as well.

"Something about him just hits me wrong, that's all. Nothing to worry about."

Eileen rubbed her hands together avariciously. "Well, that clears the field for me, then. Be back in a bit." She got up and headed over.

Izzy laughed. "Nothing will come of it. She's a flirt."

The night continued without event but with a great deal of fun and laughter, and by the time Billie was climbing into bed, she had mostly forgotten her unease. She hadn't forgotten Derik. If he was someone Erin was close to, she needed to check him out a little, so she could feel confident of her friend's safety.

CHAPTER FIVE

When Billie walked into Caleb's office the next morning, he stopped what he was doing, looked her up and down, and laughed. "How late were you out last night? You look like something the cat dragged in. Or maybe the pixie."

She dropped into the empty chair on the near side of his desk. "Shush."

His grin widened. "In other news, I hear your dancing skills are…" He paused as if searching for the right word, then finished, "Interesting."

Billie made a pistol out of her index finger and thumb and pointed it at him. "Don't make me shoot you."

"I'm shaking in my shoes right now."

She sighed dramatically. "You better hope our candidate arrives soon, or you'll be shaking, jittering, and dancing in your shoes when I blast you with lightning."

He kept grinning. "I can shield, you know."

"Not well enough."

His phone buzzed, and he picked it up. "Saved by the

bell." He departed and came back a minute later with their administrative candidate.

The latter was thin, with sharp bones in his face and a ready smile. Billie rose and extended a hand, which he shook solidly, and introduced herself.

He replied, "I'm Justin, but you already knew that."

She waved at the chair beside her, and he sat. "I did. I spent some time yesterday reading all about you, in fact. Quite a career."

As Caleb sat, he asked, "Want coffee or anything?"

Justin grinned. "Aren't I supposed to ask you that? And no, thanks." He looked at Billie, clearly unperturbed by the way she had positioned herself so he couldn't easily get both her and Caleb in the same visual field. "I started in the corporate sector. Restaurant maître d', hotel concierge. I like helping people, basically. From there, I got snapped up by the manager of the hotel as an assistant, then by one of the execs at the company."

Caleb replied, "Where they paid you better than the government does, so why the switch?"

Justin laughed. "Actually, not that much more, and the benefits here are far better. My wife is a doctor, and that pays well and is her passion, so it leaves me to do what I enjoy."

Billie asked, "So what did work at the FBI and Secret Service entail?"

"If I gave you details, I'd be in violation of my NDA. But I will say it included a variety of tasks from setting up trips to event management, procurement, and everything in between. I'm able to use some specialized equipment here and there because of it."

Billie nodded. "That's fair."

Caleb noted, "It would be a wide variety of responsibilities here. Keeping supplies up, paperwork, travel, dealing with inspections from above, hopefully warning us of inspections from above," he finished with a raised eyebrow.

Justin nodded. "I'm deep in the grapevine, no worries there. If there's a rumor, I'll hear it."

Billie was already leaning toward him, but that last comment decided her. What he didn't know, they could teach him, and he clearly had advanced skills in government politics.

They chatted about details for a while longer, then Caleb escorted him out of the building. When he came back, he got to the point. "We're hiring him, right?"

Billie nodded. "For sure. We'll let it rest today, so he doesn't think we're desperate."

Caleb laughed. "Fair. I'm sure he'll be completely fooled."

Quentin stuck his head in the door. "Got a sec?"

Billie waved at the chair. "Absolutely. We just found an admin."

The team's sniper and gunsmith grinned. "Excellent. I have some things I need them to order."

She laughed. "Of course you do."

As he took the seat, he explained, "I think I've found a demolitions expert for the team."

"I didn't know you were looking for one."

"I'm tired of being average at it. The team needs better."

Caleb remarked, "Can't argue with that."

Billie agreed. "When can we meet them?"

Quentin replied, "Today, if we can get to Atlanta before three."

"Why Atlanta?"

Mischief colored his eyes. "You'll see."

Billie turned her head to look at Caleb. "Can you work your magic and get us transport to Atlanta?"

He scratched his chin. "We're gonna have to pay these favors back, you know, boss."

"Tell whoever needs convincing that I can portal them to Vegas anytime."

Caleb laughed. "That'll get us into the green, real fast. I'll set it up."

A couple of hours, a portal, and an autonomous taxi ride later, they were in an industrial section of Atlanta, Georgia. The trucks, trailers, and abundant people running around in shirts with a movie title on them indicated the truth of the place.

Billie asked, "I suppose they use a lot of real demolitions in movies?"

Quentin replied, "They do, and the person I brought you to meet is one of the best. We have to wait until they get this shot to talk to her, though. They only have one take to get it. You'll see why."

They moved closer to the action, having acquired credentials to visit the set before arriving, and took in the scene. Several cameras were in place on a two-lane road that stretched into the distance for what looked like several miles. The nearby portion had cars on both sides, and beyond them, a massive pair of buildings with a skywalk about three stories up connecting them dominated the space. The drone-mounted cameras hovering overhead were angled to get shots of those buildings as well as the road.

Eventually, a car pulled up. Its engine growled as it idled next to the director. It looked like a muscle car from the mid-twentieth century, and Billie appreciated the aesthetic. When everything was arranged, the car drove down to the far end of the road, where it was only a small dot.

Someone announced via loudspeaker, "Quiet on the set for the rehearsal." Then the car sped down the road and skidded to a sideways stop about twenty feet away from the camera positioned in the middle of the street.

The director jogged over and said something to the driver, who turned the car and headed back to the far end. They rehearsed the move three more times before the director was satisfied.

As the person with the loudspeaker announced that the next take would be the real one, Billie asked, "What's going to happen?"

Quentin laughed. "I haven't told you yet. What makes you think I'm going to tell you now?"

"Worth a try."

Caleb advised, "They're starting."

The roar of the engine was audible in the distance as the vehicle flew down the road like it had the four previous times. Moments before it reached the two buildings, they exploded. Pieces shot in all directions except onto the street. Supplemental explosions brought both buildings down upon themselves, and the skywalk crashed onto the road only a second after the car flashed under it.

Billie whispered, "Holy hell," and was further amazed as

the cars on both sides exploded as the muscle car reached them. They flipped up into the air and over the street, landing on the opposite side but not hitting the stunt car. It skidded to a sideways stop in front of the camera as the last vehicles behind it crashed to the ground. The moment hung, then the entire crew broke into loud cheering.

Quentin informed them, "Shaped charges to control the direction of the explosions. And, of course, perfect timing."

Billie shook her head, deeply impressed. "Wow."

"Exactly. The crew has magicals as backup, but that's just in case something goes wrong."

A woman in a ponytail and one of the crew shirts came out and gave high fives to the director, the camera people, and the car's driver. Then she jogged over and punched Quentin in the shoulder. "Hey, Cue."

He rubbed it. "Hiya, Hannah. This is Billie, and Caleb."

Hannah smiled. "I've heard a lot about you."

Billie sensed the touch of the other woman's magic on hers as they shook hands. She commented, "As far as job interviews go, that was a hell of a thing."

Hannah laughed. "Killed two birds with one bomb. It took days to set it up after a bunch of computer modeling. But it worked as expected."

"You're interested in joining our team?"

"As long as I can still freelance with movies, at least with the planning and prep stuff. I could do that remotely, so I'd still be available for whatever the team needs."

Billie stated, "As long as we're first."

Hannah nodded. "Of course."

"Give Quentin your information. We'll get you vetted fast."

The other woman did so, then wandered off to get back to work.

Caleb remarked, "Being in the pressure of the moment will be different than this, what with the gunfire and bad guys and all."

Quentin replied, "She's worked extensively as an armorer for movies, too. That's how we met. She can shoot if we need her to. Plus, magic."

Billie cautioned, "Yeah. But be sure to make sure she knows everything she's getting into, Quentin."

"I already have, but I will do it again, just to be sure." He wandered off, presumably to do so.

Billie commented to Caleb, "Thinking of her joining the team reminded me of something. We need some bullet-proof shields we can carry. Something like what AET uses, but even more portable. I don't like having to rely on conveniently placed debris."

"Hard agree. I'll mention it to Eileen."

"Yeah. Do that." She looked at the destruction on the movie set and muttered, "Damn, it'll be nice having that skill on the team."

CHAPTER SIX

Onyx headed through the pixie compound hidden among the trees in the National Arboretum. She had downsized to fit into the traditionally pixie-sized tunnels. This community was made up of pixies who stayed tiny most of the time, making her the outlier since she spent most of her time in her full-size human equivalent. It made her feel "other" among those who didn't, but that was nothing new since her general behavior and attitude had accomplished the same thing most of her life, regardless of size.

In deference to the formality of an actual council meeting, she had donned a full-length tunic that resembled a dress slit up the sides to her waist. She wore shorts underneath, and her typical crisscrossing belts lay atop it. The others in the meeting room were similarly attired, although the red shade of her tunic was rather brighter than most of theirs.

The chamber was made of richly polished wood all

around with branches that wove in and out and served as irregular seating. She took her spot in the crook of one, crossed her legs, and waited for the session to begin.

Emerald, who was also a newer member of the council like Onyx, jumped up and sat beside her. "How's the outside world, Onyx?"

"Exciting. You should come out with me sometime, have an adventure."

The other woman laughed. "I'm good here, thanks." She was a chef and took part in cooking for the community. Onyx was sure she would be able to step into any fancy restaurant in the city, but that wasn't her ambition. Yet. Onyx would continue to push.

With loud claps, the elders called the meeting to order. They were in the only formal chairs in the room. While not quite thrones, the seats gave them a status that the remainder of the dozen or so attendees lacked.

Elder Brook requested, "Onyx, please tell us about your recent adventure."

Onyx had already told the elders the story and imagined that was the reason they had called this meeting. She reminded them of the initial encounter with Raffertey's brother in the warehouse and the incident in the museum, then shared the part they hadn't heard, how Billie and her team had gone after Raffertey and taken him down.

The council members were mostly silent as she shared the tale, but hushed conversations started around the room when she finished. The elders let it go on for several minutes before Elder River clapped once and asked, "Who wishes to speak?"

Gale stood. He was older than her by a decade, maybe more. His clothes were richer, his hair a respectable shade of brown, and his bearing was as upright as he was uptight.

His voice was somber as he declared, "As I have said before in these chambers, it is foolish for us to maintain an active relationship with the human government. Our lives are apart from theirs and should stay that way. Onyx should be respected for her efforts to assist the humans, and the magicals among them, but that is not a positive choice for us as a whole. It invites oversight at best and trouble at worst. We risk the entire community through this engagement."

He sat, and a different man, Torrent, stood. He was yet another decade older than the previous speaker and sported a long mane of white hair pulled back in a topknot. "With all due respect, Gale, we have discussed this issue repeatedly, and the answer has always been the same. We cannot just hide in here and pretend the outside world doesn't exist. If we do that, what's the point of being on this planet? We could go back to Oriceran and hide from all possible dangers there."

Torrent shook his head. "No. We are here for a reason—to learn, to live, to thrive. Hiding accomplishes none of these things. My concern, perhaps, is the exact opposite of yours. Are we doing enough as a community to help with the protection of our city?"

Onyx restrained herself from rolling her eyes. That was as common a refrain as Gale's insular approach was. Elder River asked Onyx, "Do you think the creation of this division, and the presence of Billie Keller to lead it, indicates a current threat to us, or to the city?"

Onyx shook her head. "I don't. That is something of a question inside the unit as well, but Billie's superior says it's not the case. Whether she's truthful or not, I cannot judge. It's always possible she doesn't have all the information since there are others superior to her. But I do not sense a threat."

Gale countered, "Yet within weeks of her arrival, a giant crystal monster decimated part of the city."

"Correlation, not causation. And we should thank the fates she and her team were here to deal with it. I'm not sure how big it would have gotten, but it didn't seem as if it was going to stop growing anytime soon."

Conversation continued for a quarter of an hour until Elder Rain clapped to stop it. She directed, "Onyx, you will keep your eye on Billie Keller."

Onyx bobbed her head in acceptance. "Of course. She's out of town today, but when she returns, I will make every effort to stay at her side."

Torrent asked, "What can we as the council do to support you?"

Onyx hadn't expected the question, but she had an answer ready to hand. "I need a bow."

Torrent smiled. He favored that weapon. "We will give you a letter to take to Ash."

"Thank you."

The council moved on to other things, and Onyx paid close attention. She and Emerald both listened much more than they spoke, each only offering a comment or two. That was the way of things in the pixie council. Longevity in the group mattered, and those with more of it did more of the talking. Arguably, it was because they were wiser, although Onyx wasn't sure that was true of all of them.

When the council finished, she returned to her room to change, then headed for an area of the community she hadn't visited often. Opening the door revealed a small room of polished wood. The far wall was not a wall but a circle etched into the wood. The outer rim was exquisitely engraved with ornate glyphs and sigils. She reached for her belt, pulled off a stud that contained magically charged dust, and blew it at the circle.

At its touch, the ring activated. Each of the sigils glowed to life, and when all were illuminated, the wooden interior vanished to reveal a village on the far side. Onyx stepped through the opening and moved from Earth to Oriceran. Once across, she used her magic to grow to human size because this village had opted to live that way.

A curving path led toward the buildings, and she smiled at the idyllic scene as she walked, basking in the perfect sunshine-filled weather. Rolling fields stretched out to both sides, and ahead was a forest that was no longer a forest as such.

The trees had been nurtured and altered to create buildings on both sides of the path. Generations upon generations had worked to craft this place from the living wood, and further generations would continue to maintain and expand it. It was her home, although she rarely visited it anymore. She noted the fans moving lazily to create comfortable breezes, fueled by magic, as was everything in the village since that power was abundant on the magical planet, unlike on Earth.

About a quarter of the way along the path, she reached

Ash's home and workshop. She entered and discovered him seated in a comfortable chair, turning the pages of a book with an ornate cover. He smiled and stood as she approached, then opened his arms. She hugged him. "Uncle Ash."

"Niece. How are you?"

"Very well. I've come to make a bow." She extended the letter.

He read it, and raised his eyebrow at the end. "Well, the elders don't mince words. We're supposed to do this immediately." He looked at her. "Are you in danger? Is the community?"

Onyx shook her head. "Not as such. It's nothing to worry about and would take too long to explain."

"All right. I'll accept that for now. Come into the back."

His spotless workshop contained hand tools of every description, all of which would be supplemented by his magic skills, which he'd trained over the years in the craft of manipulating wood. She'd seen him reshape a branch with seeming effortlessness on any number of occasions. Once, she'd thought that might be her path as well, but as yet it had not turned out that way.

He examined a collection of wooden pieces already shaped into bows, and had her hold several until he found the one he thought was the right size and weight for her. He strung it, had her pull on it, and nodded approval at the thwack of the string's release. Then he led her to a table and sat across it from her. "The bow will, of course, be charmed for accuracy. What else would you like, if anything?"

She considered the last battle. "Solidity, so it resists damage."

"From?"

"Everything."

Ash chuckled. "You will definitely need to tell me that tale. All right, place your fingers on the wood." She set them at one end. His touched hers, fingertip to fingertip, and his magic wrapped around the bow and her hands. He began to chant, and as he moved his hands down the wood, hers moved with them without any effort on her part.

They spent an hour caressing the wood, and when they were done, it was deeply polished and every inch of it covered in glyphs and designs. Again, he had her try it out and broke into a broad grin. "Perfect. You have always had a talent for woodwork."

Onyx countered, "You did it all."

"We did it. And you have talent. Don't argue. What kind of arrows would you like?"

She considered the question. "Lightning, fire, and explosive."

He raised a bushy eyebrow. "Explosive?"

"Sometimes we face powerful enemies."

They spent another hour crafting them with her setting her magic into each so she would know the type by touch. When it was over, he offered, "I will send more with my next shipment to your community."

She hugged him again. "Thank you, uncle."

"Just promise me you're not going to use them for something stupid that gets you into trouble."

Onyx laughed. "You know I can't do that. It wouldn't be any fun."

His grin matched hers. "You wouldn't be you if you could. Stay safe and come back when you're ready to really learn how to woodcraft."

She waved. Maybe one day she would, but today wasn't that day. Today, she had to get back to Billie before the other woman found something exciting to do and she missed it.

CHAPTER SEVEN

The next morning, Billie headed up to the top of the building for a meeting with her boss, Helen Flores. When she arrived, she encountered a man seated across the desk from Helen.

He rose and extended a hand. "Arthur Blackwood." His accent was English, and his look seemed to proclaim his origins equally well. He was a little over six feet tall, trim, and athletic. The lighter part of his perfectly styled salt and pepper hair was a shade darker than his pale skin, but just that. His confidence suggested he knew he was handsome but didn't care much about it.

She shook it and took the seat beside him as he sat.

Helen explained, "Arthur runs a specialized security company that protects its clients from magical threats. It made sense that you two should meet."

He added, "It's called Spellbound Security. We have busy offices in Los Angeles, Miami, and Cleveland, plus a couple other locations that are less successful and might have been bad choices on my part." He chuckled.

Billie wasn't sure how friendly Helen wanted her to be, so she kept her tone and content neutral. "Do you have specific concerns we can assist with?"

He waved off her concern. "Not at the moment. But my people often come up against, shall we say, *impressive* opposition. I thought it would make sense for a channel between us to already exist when and if that happened again."

Helen added, "Basically, he's looking for help on the government's dime."

Blackwood laughed. "Guilty as charged. I'm always working the angles for my people."

Helen countered, "For your pocketbook."

"For both."

Billie nodded. "Well, that is kind of our mandate."

Helen's tone turned serious. "Arthur and his people have encountered some fairly organized opposition, which is at least at the boundary of what we do."

"I'd say that's right in the crosshairs of what we do."

Arthur volunteered, "I brought you a list of the infomancers for each of my offices. My people thought that was probably the best way to share information on a casual basis. If we need to deepen the conversation, they have your number."

Billie accepted the list. "Sounds good to me. I'll pass this along to my infomancer right away."

Blackwood grinned. "I couldn't ask for more."

Helen laughed again. "Oh, he'll find something to complain about, be sure of it."

Billie left the bantering pair behind and took the elevator down to her unit's level. Izzy's office was her first stop, and the infomancer was behind her desk as usual. She explained the meeting and handed over the list. The corner of Izzy's mouth quirked as she read it, and Billie asked, "Why the amusement?"

"I've heard of some of these folks, is all. The ones I know are sharp."

"Good. Maybe consider how we can expand our alert network. Are there other organizations that could feed us information about growing threats?"

Izzy shook her head with a dubious expression. "You're opening a can of worms there if you go too far. Conspiracy theorists abound."

Billie smiled. "I'll trust you to sort the wheat from the chaff."

The infomancer lifted her eyes to the ceiling in a long-suffering expression. "Gee, thanks, boss."

"Don't mention it."

Billie lost herself in paperwork, time passing until Anya and Onyx walked into her office together and asked, "Are you ready? You were supposed to meet us in the lobby."

Billie looked at the time. "Sorry about that. Yeah, let's go."

They took one of the SUVs from the garage one level up and drove out to the suburbs, to Ethan and Elaine's shop. As they climbed out of the car, Anya commented, "Okay, that's adorable."

Billie agreed. "It really is."

There were shops on either side that were normal-looking, appropriate to the day and age. Ethan's store, Oddities and Enticements, was not. An old-style wooden sign dominated the façade with a glass window underneath it. Inside the window was a forest scene with magical creatures everywhere one looked.

A bell rang as they headed inside, and Elaine looked up from the counter. She smiled as she recognized them. "Billie, who are your friends?"

Billie introduced Onyx and Anya as she approached the counter. It was wood, polished to a shining glow.

Elaine explained, "Since it's your first time here, I'll give you the lowdown. Over on those racks are our potions." She gestured to her right. "They're all recently made, so they're at full potency, which is why you won't see too many of them. Ethan doesn't like to waste components."

Onyx observed, "Smart."

Elaine favored the pixie with a smile. "Over there, you'll find charms of every type. Some are decorative, others are magical. Of course, they wouldn't be as powerful as ones you might craft yourself from an attunement perspective, but they can still be handy to have around."

Then she smiled broadly. "Behind you are our magical toys. That's what Ethan and I love best. Probably you don't need them, but they make excellent gifts, especially if you can top them up now and again with your magic to keep them running."

All three of them went to that section and found puppets, cars, trains, and an assortment of other items. Each came to life when touched with magic. The puppets in particular were impressive, waving their arms in gestures that looked very human.

Billie remarked, "Not today, but sometime, for sure."

A man called a muffled, "Who's there?"

Elaine shouted, "Billie Keller and friends."

"Send them back."

Elaine rolled her eyes. "He wants to show off. Be kind."

All three of them were laughing as they headed through the door at the back of the shop. Beyond it was a medium-sized room filled with alchemical equipment. Billie recognized the burners, mortars, and pestles easily but totally failed to understand a half-dozen other objects that looked as if they contributed to the creation of the objects in the outer room.

Ethan wiped off his hands on his apron and shook her hand with both of his. "Billie, I'm so glad you came. And you all, as well. Did you like the toys?"

She laughed. "I love the toys. They are amazing."

His grin broadened. "They make great gifts."

"When I have an occasion to buy a gift, this will definitely be my first stop. Today we're here for potions."

"What kinds?"

Anya replied, "Healing and energy."

He headed to a rack and pulled out two of each, then looked at Onyx. "Do these work on you?"

She shrugged. "I've never tried."

He handed her a small bottle with a cork on the top and the familiar red healing liquid inside it. "The next time you scratch yourself, give it a try. If it works, great. If not, you can come in and we can see if we can figure out a formula that will work for you."

She accepted it and tucked it into her belt with a thank you.

Billie asked, "Do you have other kinds?"

He chuckled. "Of course. I'm always experimenting.

The two kinds that work best are the ones that amplify senses, and the one that allows mind reading."

Anya replied, "Mind reading? Next you're going to say love potions."

He pointed with an exaggerated scowl. "No reputable potion maker would do love potions. Aphrodisiacs, now, different story." He cackled.

"It's not technically mind reading. It's more being open to all the information another person is giving off. Their auras, their micro-level movements, et cetera. It's not perfect, but it has some utility. I don't sell it to gamblers or people engaged in competitive sports for obvious reasons."

Billie nodded, thinking that such a thing would be handy for investigative purposes, and filed that away. "We'll stick with these for now."

Ethan laughed. "Elaine will settle up with you at the front counter." He whispered faux-conspiratorially, "I have some hallucinogens, if you're interested."

His grin was infectious. She replied, "Maybe for the weekend."

He laughed again. "Sure, sure. See you soon."

As they left the building, Onyx commented, "You know, if you want hallucinogens, I know a source." She referred to one of the varieties of dust she carried.

Billie scowled at the pixie. "I don't want hallucinogens."

"It's just that it keeps coming up."

"Because you keep bringing it up. Hush."

Onyx laughed and continued to harass her about the hallucinogens all the way back to their building.

CHAPTER EIGHT

E ileen looked around her lab in satisfaction. She'd had many before, but this one was her favorite. The newest usually was since the space included the tools and techniques she had improved over time, and was usually outfitted exactly as she liked it. That autonomy had been one of her conditions for coming over to the new unit at Helen's request, although she was sure Billie would have given it the thumbs-up as well if needed.

The lab contained three high, six-foot-long worktables that she could sit in front of with her rolling chair or stand comfortably at to work. Large tools on telescoping arms were mounted on a grid of rails in the ceiling that allowed them access to the entire space, and a tall rolling mechanic's toolkit at each of the tables held an array of tools for specific projects that could be moved from one table to another as needed.

The fourth wall was dedicated to an elaborate computer workstation. The high-end machine could handle every step of the process from research through prototype. Currently, Izzy was seated there. Today's dress was a deep red, almost brown, with long sleeves that fell past her fingertips.

Eileen was occasionally jealous of her friend's good looks and ostentatious dress. She'd tried pulling off more exaggerated looks in the past, but they never made her feel like herself. So, she might not be one to turn heads, but she was happy and in her element, which mattered far more.

Izzy asked, "Are you planning to just stare at the ceiling, or do you think you might do some actual work?"

Eileen scowled across the room. "Maybe you should get that AI finished and mind your own business."

"It's compiling. And you're delaying." The infomancer stood, stretched, and walked across the room to stand with her at the table. She gestured at the large drone that took up most of the available space on the tabletop. "Do you need my help?"

"No. It has all the stuff you wanted. Better rockets, with multiple targeting modes. Selectable ammo feeds for the cannon." She pointed at the two ammo boxes, both of which fed into the rotating gun on the front. She'd had to rebuild the frame and upgrade the engines to accommodate the extra weight.

"And the defenses?"

"Chaff dispenser on the back, hardened skin, and hopefully improved evasion from your AI, if it works."

"Oh, it'll work."

Eileen tapped a finger against her teeth, an annoying habit she hadn't yet been able to break. "As I recall, there was some previous use of the drones for ramming purposes."

Izzy patted the drone as if it was a pet. "You recall correctly."

"It would be nice if you didn't demolish this one that way."

The infomancer shrugged, looking not at all apologetic. "Sometimes, that's the only option."

Eileen pointed to two spots next to the cannon. "What if we mounted blades here and here that would extend and join together? Create a kind of lance?"

Izzy stared down at it. "Three or four would be better. More supportive."

"Agree. We'd have to pull the gun back a little, but I think there's room." Eileen grabbed the tablet next to the drone, called up the schematics, and projected them into the air. She moved pieces around until finally the image glowed green, telling her that the computer inside thought her modifications would work.

Izzy nodded. "Looks like a big improvement to me. Get it to work, and I'll take you out for drinks. How's the stealth model?"

Eileen gestured at another table. "That one still needs some work, but the primary components are in place. We have expanded sensors, a high-powered infomancer relay, minimal noise motors, and a special skin that should keep it from being detected. I gotta tell you, the material to make that skin is super expensive and not readily available."

"Ideally, we'll only need one at a time."

"Not have a backup? Are you crazy?"

Izzy laughed. "Do what you need to do. I can rob a bank if you need more money."

Eileen rolled her eyes. "Maybe embezzle from the international division. They have too many resources anyway."

Billie walked into the room. "Who's embezzling what?"

Eileen and Izzy laughed at her, but neither offered an explanation.

Billie gestured at the objects on the tables. "What do we have here?"

Eileen explained the drones. "As long as the AI works, it should be a great asset if you ever come up against something like the Crystal Colossus again."

Billie winced. "Don't even whisper that possibility."

Izzy asked, "Getting superstitious, boss?"

"After almost getting stepped on by a creature as big as a building? Yes. Yes, I am."

Eileen replied, "Then this might interest you." The team's research tech headed to a cabinet and came back with two handfuls of the red metal plates that the team used for armor. She set them on the table and tapped one. They snapped together to form a two-deep rectangle.

Billie said, "Impressive. What's it for?"

"Eventually, I hope we can use it to build an exoskeleton. Small actuators and even smaller batteries, but if we put them all together, they might give us a substantial increase in strength."

"That would be handy, especially for the team members who can't do it with magic."

"Exactly what I was thinking."

Eileen took them back to the cabinet and brought back another set. They looked slightly different and were arranged in a brick, about twice the size of a pack of cards and slightly larger.

Billie asked, "Another set of actuators?"

"Kind of." Eileen tapped some items on the tablet, and the bricks moved.

Billie noticed that they were much smaller than their normal plates as they reconfigured themselves into a small craft complete with tiny turbo fans. "Miniature drone?"

"Yep."

It was triangular with three fans driving it. The craft moved back and forth through the air, spinning as it climbed and descended.

Izzy explained, "It has cameras and audio sensors at the moment. We might be able to stick more things in it eventually, but it'll give us more eyes and ears in the field. The same AI we're using for the combat drones will control it."

Eileen added, "We'll probably want to stick that in the stealth drones, eventually, too."

Billie asked, "Any weapons in the little one?"

"No, but you could ram it into someone, I suppose."

Izzy laughed. "Then she'd give you hell when you got back for damaging her toys."

Eileen snapped, "Shush."

It landed and folded back up into its dormant state. Billie lifted it to assess the weight. "Nice and light. This is great work."

A chime from the far end of the room drew all their attention, then a voice came out of the speakers mounted on the computer. "Greetings. I am Andi. Please tell me how I can serve."

Izzy clapped. "All right. AI in the house."

Eileen sighed and looked at Billie. "I have a bad feeling about this."

CHAPTER NINE

Izzy sipped from a can of cold brew coffee as she settled in front of her home computer system. She was staying in this Friday night, opting to confine her social engagements to the magical dark web. She logged into her system and activated the customized avatar and outfit she used for relaxing as Alloy. It lacked a majority of the tools and abilities that she carried on actual work, but she knew she wouldn't run into trouble in the places she would visit that night, nor would she have to make her way through any security levels. She was well-known and had earned the right to bypass the minor checks that most infomancers had to go through, and her basic generic loadout would handle whatever else might be needed.

Izzy finished her drink, leaned forward in her chair, and closed her eyes. The magical dark web appeared in front of her, and she headed to her first stop, Rogue. She spent an agreeable hour inside, chatting with people she'd talked to or played video games against before. Then she headed to her second stop of the night, Ronaldo's.

The place looked like a dive bar from the outside, and the first impression over the threshold was the same. Talented infomancers saw beyond that illusion to the subdued lighting, understated neon signs, and comfortable leather furniture. The glass bar featured tropical fish swimming beneath the flat top, which served as both an interface and a display.

Alloy was moderately surprised to see one of her favorite contacts already seated at the bar. She sat at the bar beside the other woman, whose avatar looked as if it had been yanked out of a cyberpunk video game, right down to the spiked hair that stuck out in all directions. She laughed internally because Voltaic's name had been on the list of infomancers she'd gotten. She had wondered if they would wind up working together with her in her FBI capacity.

That didn't worry her. She kept the behaviors of both her identities carefully separate. This one was far more like her. "May I say, you're looking scorching tonight, befitting your name."

Voltaic rolled her eyes as she always did when Izzy-as-Alloy flirted with her. It was a great technique for setting other infomancers off their guard, and she used it constantly, perhaps even recklessly. Plus, it was fun. Voltaic replied, "Looking for you, actually."

"Well, what did I do to deserve such attention?"

Voltaic shook her head with a laugh. "Settle down, woman. I need you for a run tonight. Planning to go in around two."

Alloy nodded. "Work, or freelance?" She had helped the other infomancer with runs of both kinds before.

"Work. We have some espionage that turned nasty."

"I thought you people were more personal security than corporate." She knew some details from having assisted Spellbound before.

"Someone tried to kill the CEO today by blowing up his car with a fireball."

Alloy winced. "Well, I see your concern, then. Of course I'm in." When she had the address, she logged out, then headed to bed. A nap would be useful since infomancy runs could be minutes or hours, depending on the complexities involved.

When she woke up, she showered, dressed, and logged into her computers again. As always, her first task was to ensure her reroutings were all functioning as expected. They kept her safe by preventing enemies from tracking her back to her location in the real world. Again, Alloy used a different set than her FBI identity, Nakano. When she was confident her security was unchanged, she logged into her arming room.

An expanse of whiteness extended in all directions. At her arrival, columns rose from the floor or descended from above, floating into place on a specific path. She walked along the curving area between them to collect her gear. The first one had a shelf that supported the cuffs of her samurai armor, pure silver that shimmered as if they were freshly polished.

She set them in place on her wrists and ankles, and the armor awoke from its somnolence. Metal crawled out from them to cover her skin with fine scales. The colors of the armor changed depending on her mental state, and this time they shone black with emblems in scarlet running down her spine, arms, and legs. Red always indicated an anticipation of battle to come, a representation of virtual blood that would be spilled.

The scales covered her up to her throat, ending just below her jaw. A mental command activated the test process, and the armor flexed and writhed as the tiny detachable robots that made it up tested their individual functions. Upon completion without errors, another mental command extended spikes from her toes and heels, then retracted them.

Alloy went to the next pedestal, which contained her weapons. The first was a star-shaped buckle that snapped into place on the suit's belt. Next, she slipped ornamental caps over each knuckle on her gauntlets. Finally, she took her daishō from the column that supported the twin swords and sheathed them in the receptacles on the back of her armor. She didn't need to test the draw. It was always perfect.

A little farther on, shelves in one of the columns supported a variety of grenades. She selected as many as would fit on her belt. They looked like integral pieces of the armor, which she thought helped to add to the surprise when she threw them at an opponent. Finally, she selected narrow silver pins about twice as long as her index finger from the next column and inserted them into the long hair that hung down to the middle of her back.

With that complete, she held up her palm. The gauntlet created a holographic image of her. As it rotated in place, she checked to ensure her hair was as it should be, her armor looked right, and the metal covering half of her face was perfect. It all was, as it always was. She was ready.

With a wave, she banished the image and jumped into the air. The room dissolved around her, replaced by the magical dark web. She descended slowly to land at the spot Voltaic had shared. The other woman was already there.

In front of them was an old-looking building constructed of large stone blocks with dirty mortar in between. Square glass panes filled an arched entrance except for where a set of eight doors allowed human avatars representing data to move in and out. The data wore dated but affluent clothing, like something from a world sometime before computers, which matched the architecture.

Izzy noted, "That's different. A train station. Let me guess, transportation company?"

Voltaic nodded. "Historically."

"Now?"

"Pharmaceuticals. They're part of the race to use extra-planetary materials to make new drugs."

It wasn't a large leap to the next conclusion. Alloy observed, "If I'm not mistaken, that's the business the executive you're protecting is in."

Voltaic imitated a carnival game operator. "The little lady wins a prize."

Alloy gestured at the doors. "No time like the present."

"Agreed."

"After you."

Voltaic grinned. "No, after you."

Alloy replied, "I insist," finishing the ritual they often invoked at the start of a mission. Laughing, they headed for the doors side by side.

CHAPTER TEN

The train station's interior was far larger than Alloy had expected it would be despite the glass exterior showing its size. Her mind had apparently not filled in that the whole place was that large. Birds flew above, flitting from one dangling ceiling fan to the next, cawing their annoyance at the passengers flocking below. She observed, "Nice touch."

Voltaic pointed. "That too." In a corner, a 1920s-style newsboy in a baker boy cap held out broadsheets filled with garish tabloid fare as he called out the news of the day.

Alloy observed, "Content's not much different than now."

"You spend too much time on social media."

"That's where all the cute people are. You should join."

"Stop." Voltaic couldn't smother her smile.

Alloy laughed inwardly. She loved teasing the other infomancer. They moved cautiously through the space, surrounded by data that flowed in all directions. Three different descending staircases and escalators exited, one to the left, one to the right, and one ahead. The data seemed confused about which one to go to, milling around in the center before eventually choosing a path.

Voltaic observed, "Looks to me like we need to go straight ahead."

"Agreed."

That was where most of the data with a specific purpose seemed to be heading. As they angled in that direction, Alloy felt a warning tingle on the back of her neck as her systems pinged her that something needed her attention. She found the telltale immediately. Security had begun to move. The blue-uniformed officers around the room's periphery sauntered more or less in their direction.

She opened her mouth to speak, but Voltaic muttered, "I see them. We should probably thin their numbers out some before we move on."

"Always bad to leave an enemy at your back."

"You handle your side, I'll handle mine."

Alloy smiled smugly. "And once I'm done with mine, I'll come help you with yours."

Voltaic laughed. "You're such a cocky wench."

"Truth." She dashed to the left in an effort to draw those nearest their ultimate destination away from it. The guards had pistols in wide leather belts, and while each had removed the safety strap, none had yet drawn them. Their symmetrical motions revealed their lack of sophistication, and she categorized them as low-level bots. Not a threat, but a potential annoyance.

Alloy momentarily considered ignoring them, but the opportunity had passed. Eight of them were within ten feet of her. She activated her predictive software, a custom piece of code that she had written long ago and continuously refined with every infomancy run since. It projected colored paths of likely movements of her enemies, and also her allies if she had worked with them often enough, as she had with Voltaic.

Her system updated the probabilities of her enemies' actions from moment to moment, creating a visual cacophony that only endless practice allowed her to interpret. In a way, it was like seeing multiple paths in the future and choosing among them, or that was how a science fiction movie might describe it.

Thinking time ended, and action time began. Alloy's blades rasped out as she drew them from their metallic sheaths. The larger katana was in her right hand, and the smaller wakizashi in her left.

The closest enemy on her right happened to be one step nearer than the one on the left, which earned him the opportunity to be the first to die. She spun to face him and stabbed forward with her off hand blade. It rammed into his chest, causing him to break up into pixels and fall away. She continued the spin, which ended in a backhand stab into the chest of the next nearest. He, too, vanished.

Alloy was already moving toward the two across from her as all of the bots pulled their pistols at the same time. She leapt on a trajectory that carried her between them and slashed both blades out to the sides, decapitating each bot. Their bodies vanished before any part of them hit the floor.

She landed, rolled, and came up in a crouch. Bullets that would have connected if she'd stood passed over her head and struck several pieces of data that fell before they vanished. She thought that was an interesting wrinkle since normally simulations didn't allow data to be impacted by fighting going on in the server.

Alloy ran to her left, toward the next nearest, neatly putting them in the path of any bullets from the far ones. The bots shot anyway, their synchronicity allowing them to aim past their allies. Her predictive systems allowed her to lean out of the way of those she could avoid and flick up her blades to block the others.

A double diagonal slash took out the next guard, and she leapt up, spun, and kicked the one behind him in the head. A bullet clipped her shoulder as he fell, but her armor protected her from anything more than a light bruise.

Several more slashes, and her enemies were down. She turned to see if Voltaic needed assistance, but the gunfire that had been going off continuously in the background had taken care of her partner's foes. Alloy commented, "That wasn't hard."

Voltaic looked back toward the doors through which they entered. "But here come reinforcements. I think we should get below."

"Agreed." Alloy ran toward the escalators and jumped onto the metal ramp between them. She slid down on her backside with her legs out straight, keeping her eyes focused below. It was a long descent, with a slight level portion in the middle that caused her to fly into the air before crashing down again, and it gave her plenty of time to see the enemies waiting for them below. They were dressed as security guards as well, but they had pistols and batons, both of them drawn.

She activated a consumable shield, one of a few she carried, and it absorbed the damage from the bullets as they struck her during the last part of her slide. As her boots hit the floor, she was ready and able to dish out a little of what she'd received. Batons deflected her slashes at the nearest pair, and they fired their guns again. Her shield dissipated as it absorbed the impacts, and she spun to the side to avoid the next barrage.

A mental command activated the small covers on her knuckles, which flew off and transformed into darts as they hurtled toward her enemies. The predictive systems had already sketched in her foes' likely paths, and the way she had positioned her fingers caused the darts to intercept them perfectly, striking vulnerable spots and removing them from the fight. It took hardly any time before the first wave was down, but another had arrived at their heels. She ran to stand beside Voltaic. "These idiots are costing us time."

The other woman nodded. "Agreed. Let's take them out before they get close."

Alloy sheathed her weapons, slipped her hands into her suit, and pulled out the throwing knives sheathed there. Three of the four buried themselves in the throats of the oncoming guards. The fourth missed, leaving her with three opponents.

Voltaic threw throwing stars with her right hand, drawing them one after the next from a holder on her left wrist. They flew true in half the cases, leaving her with three opponents as well.

Since she was out of throwing knives, Alloy reached for the long needles in her braided hair, pulled them out, and threw them. They were overkill for this level of opponent, but it couldn't be helped. A short time later, all of their enemies were down. Voltaic had switched to the dart launcher on her right arm to finish off the last couple. No reinforcements immediately appeared. Alloy asked, "All right, where to next?"

"Not sure. We have four trains to the left and five to the right, looks like."

Alloy peered around and came to the same count. Data was moving into each of them via a door in the passengers' cars halfway through the long trains. The simulation had probably been modeled against a European- or Asian-style station since she had never seen one quite this big in America firsthand. Still, pictures of the Chicago rail yards certainly rivaled it in size.

Alloy held out her left hand, palm up. Several of the pieces of metal on her gauntlet floated up and reformed themselves into a scanning device. It lifted off and stopped in a hover over the first train to the left, then deployed a red scanning beam as it flew down the length of the train. Voltaic was doing something similar to her right but without the floating sensor.

The process took too long, and Alloy's gaze constantly roamed in search of additional enemies. None came, and finally they agreed that the third train to the right was the correct one to find the data Voltaic sought. They jumped down onto the tracks, and Voltaic led the way to the rear of the train.

Alloy asked, "Don't want to enter with the passengers?"

"I'm guessing the passengers have guards guarding them."

"You think the baggage and storage cars won't?"

"I think it's less likely."

Alloy shrugged. "It's your run, sweetheart. You lead, I'll follow. You look good from this angle, by the way. Have you been working out?"

Voltaic uttered something between a groan and a sigh, opened the door to the baggage car, and led the way in. As soon as the door clanged closed at their backs, a huge cage materialized around them. The iron bars were only a hand span apart. Alloy looked back to see that the door they'd entered through was now gone.

From ahead of them came laughter, and a man in a suit with a narrow tie and a cane in his hand stepped into view. "Well done. Stupid people always come in through the back."

CHAPTER ELEVEN

As Voltaic spat curses involving irregularities in the enemy infomancer's lineage at him, Alloy activated her analysis program. The small unit lifted from her palm and spun in place, scanning the bars. She noted, "Iron mix, susceptible to high heat."

The infomancer laughed and waggled his cane. "You're not getting out that easily."

Voltaic countered, "Watch us," and drew a knife.

Alloy sent away more of the tiny robots that made up her armor. The shards of metal passed through the openings in the bars and created a cloud around the enemy infomancer. They were unlikely to do any real damage, but she hoped they would buy them some time to escape the simple, effective, and deeply annoying trap.

He threw two hissing canisters to the floor that spewed smoke through the car, blocking her sight of him.

Voltaic pressed the tip of her knife against the bar, and both the knife and the metal glowed cherry red at the point of contact. Alloy tweaked her analysis in search of a lock or trigger mechanism, and her small device whirled through the entirety of the cage before reporting back that there was no such thing available.

She crouched, grabbed the bars as best she could, and tried to lift them using her muscles plus an assist from the suit. She had lost some of her enhanced strength with the pieces she'd sent away but sensed that even at full power, she would have failed to budge the metal. She growled, "No joy," as she stood.

If they had no other option, she could have overloaded her armor until it broke down or depleted the power cells that drove it, but for now, she hoped Voltaic's method would work. The other woman was already pressing the glowing blade to a different section of the bar, and a moment later, a large piece dropped away.

One or more bars would have to come off before either of them could squeeze through the opening, but it was large enough for Alloy to try something else. She detached her star-shaped belt buckle, set it horizontally on an upraised finger, and spun it. It gained momentum as it rotated until it was whirring like a circular saw blade. She chambered her arm and threw it, twisting at the release to send it diagonally through the opening, which wasn't large enough to admit it horizontally yet. She chided herself inwardly for not making it possible to throw the blade vertically and would fix that at her earliest opportunity.

It flew across the car and into the cloud of smoke hovering around the enemy infomancer. She wasn't posi-tive of his location since the smoke obscured normal sight, and the car was somehow interfering with her thermal and sonic detection modes, giving her multiple readings that showed up as overlapping blobs in her vision. She heard an impact, but the timing didn't seem right for her to have hit the infomancer.

The second piece of metal fell away, and Voltaic climbed through, careful to avoid the glowing metal edges. Alloy followed quickly, scorching her armor as it met one of those hot spots. She gave the command to call her robots back from the pool of swirling smoke as she drew her swords. None responded, and she advanced cautiously, her daishō positioned for defense against a surprise attack.

She didn't find the infomancer, but she discovered puddles of metal on the floor that were the only remains of the robots she'd sent at him. She snarled, "He's making us spend resources. Jerk."

Voltaic replied, "Having smart enemies sucks. I wonder where he went. Sneaky bastard."

Alloy stalked to the far end of the car, where the full-size saw blade was embedded in the wall next to the door. It required some unexpected effort to tug it out after she sheathed her swords. The impact had bent it out of shape, and a quick scan showed it would neither shrink nor spin properly. She tossed it aside, lacking the time to deal with it at the moment. "So, I guess we pursue him?"

Voltaic positioned herself near the car's front door. "Yeah. But this time, no need to sneak." She yanked the door open, but it only revealed an opening between train cars and another door. Alloy saw a sliver of the landscape as it flashed by while Voltaic tossed grenades that stuck to the next barrier. Her partner asked, "Ready?"

Alloy primed herself to move. "Totally ready." She was already in motion as the explosives went off and jumped across the opening. As soon as her boots hit the floor in the next car, she threw herself forward and to the side in a shoulder roll. She sensed rather than saw something whiz past her and twisted to see Voltaic flying backward into the empty space where the car they had been in no longer was.

Alloy activated the grapnel function of her armor, which used more metal scales to launch a line with a magnetic connector on the end toward the other woman. Voltaic grabbed it with a rope of her own, and Alloy yanked her back in. She paid a price for the rescue as bullets slammed into her back, each like an angry punch from a yeti, but the armor stopped them from penetrating. She scuttled forward to crouch behind Voltaic as she assessed the damage.

She had lost a lot of her armor, which also meant she'd lost a lot of the functionality that she used to fight. The damage slowed her processes, which meant the other info-mancer would be that much quicker than she. She snarled, "I'll just have to win with skill, then," and rushed forward while yanking her swords from their sheaths. She passed shocked-looking avatars of data that sat on both sides of the passenger car but barely saw them as she focused on the tactical situation.

Her predictive software showed possibilities, but as she closed toward where Voltaic and the enemy infomancer fought at the far end of the car, she noted their foe's actions didn't match the predictions well. It wasn't something she had encountered before, and she wondered if he had a randomizer function running, or if her systems were more degraded in this place than she thought.

Voltaic was attacking with knives, not the ones she'd

used to cut through the bars, but standard combat versions Alloy recognized. The enemy infomancer had discarded his cloak and cane, revealing his dark body armor that looked like a blend of metal and polymer of some kind. Metal vambraces covered his forearms and shrouded his shins, and he moved with obvious skill as he used them to block the stabs and slashes Voltaic threw at him.

Alloy crashed down on him in silence, aiming both of her swords for the join where his neck met his right shoulder. He shocked her by spinning out of the way at the last instant, the move so fast neither she nor her predictive systems anticipated it. He ended the spin by throwing a gauntleted backfist at her face that she barely leaned back enough to avoid. His metal-covered shin slammed into hers, and she staggered back a step as she regained her balance.

Voltaic used the moment to stab at him, but he dropped an elbow down on her partner's forearm. A snapping sound shocked Alloy, and Voltaic fell back, dropping her remaining knife as she cradled the broken forearm.

Alloy growled, "Ridiculous," and fluidly retrieved and threw several grenades. Smoke, flame, light, sound, and fragments blasted the end of the car, momentarily obscuring him from view. When the conflagration cleared, two of him stood side by side. She snarled, "No way."

Both versions of him laughed. "Definitely yes way."

She threw herself into the attack and discovered, as she had hoped, that he was slower as a dual entity since his processing power was split rather than doubled. The fight moved back and forth through the car. Her sword slashes gouges in passenger seats, and his attacks with the pistols he drew from nowhere shot holes in the walls. Data took hits and died, and the blurred outside was visible through holes in the car's skin.

Alloy closed on one figure, and Voltaic moved at the other. The gunplay stopped as the pistols transformed into daggers. That gave her the advantage of reach, and she pressed her enemy toward the front of the car again. Voltaic shouted in triumph behind her, and Alloy grunted as the one she was fighting became stronger and faster. The other woman joined her, and together they boxed him in at the end of the car.

His lips twisted in a snarl as they pressed him. He reached for his belt with his free hand, then threw something to the floor. A loud explosion blew off the car's front wall as well as part of the roof.

Alloy instinctively recoiled from the detonation, and when she spotted him again, he was on top of the next car and running forward.

Voltaic panted. "You've got to be kidding me."

"You bring me to the best places." Alloy sheathed her swords, activated the much-reduced enhanced strength in her armor, and used it to leap to the top of the car. She immediately flopped down to the deck and rolled to the right as gun turrets she hadn't seen fired at her.

The move carried her over the side, and she rearranged her armor again to create claws on her gauntlets that she punched into the side of the car. Muttering several unsavory things under her breath, she used the claws to punch along the side of the car until she was even with the turrets.

Alloy used the suit's enhanced strength to leap up and

land on top of the nearest gun. She drew her katana and drove it down into the turret, which sparked and died. The other one blew up a moment later, a victim of Voltaic's hand grenades. They advanced together in silence to the end of the car. One more remained between them and the engine, and their enemy stood halfway across it with that arrogant smile still on his face. He reached out and curled his fingers back, beckoning them forward.

Voltaic raised a hand to cover her mouth. "I'll shoot high, you go low."

Alloy replied, "Works for me." She jumped over the intervening space as Voltaic's guns barked. Their enemy returned fire, and the angles the bullets took in Alloy's predictive software suggested Voltaic was also charging. The enemy infomancer was moving more or less as the software expected him to, as if it had finally processed his earlier actions. The analysis gave her an idea.

She feigned tripping as she reached melee range and rolled forward on her shoulder. He stepped forward as her software indicated he would, about to kick her as hard as possible, but she whipped out her sword and smashed it into his shin with all the power she could muster. The blow knocked him off-balance, and he staggered backward.

Alloy spun up in a single fluid move and slashed her sword across at head height. He jumped backward to avoid the blow, which allowed several of Voltaic's rounds that had probably been aimed at his head to take him in the chest.

He landed hard, but unexpectedly, didn't pixel out. Alloy walked toward him with her swords raised in guard position, and Voltaic fell in place at her side with her pistols pointed down at him. He was breathing shallowly but not moving.

Voltaic remarked, "I think he's done."

"I think you're right."

The other woman knelt, searched him, and held up a memory stick. "Got it."

Alloy lowered her wakizashi to point at the device. "You're going to share, right?"

Voltaic laughed. "Of course not. Why would I do that?"

Alloy offered a sly smile. "Because I'm pretty, and a great kisser?"

Voltaic laughed. "Yeah, that's not going to make me share data."

"Rude. Can I at least kill him?"

"Absolutely."

Alloy raised both her sword hilts high, then drove the blades down through him and into the roof of the car. He pixelated away without a sound. "Ahh, so satisfying." She sheathed the weapons.

Voltaic commented, "Thanks for the help."

"You're welcome, and you owe me."

Voltaic laughed. "As always. Talk soon, Alloy."

Alloy laughed under her breath. *Sooner than you think, I'm guessing.*

CHAPTER TWELVE

Billie had been waiting for Saturday night to arrive with a combination of excitement and trepidation. Owen had prodded her about the date he claimed she owed him earlier in the week, and they'd settled on Saturday. She had spent the day running, cleaning, and wandering, more or less, with her mind focused on the evening ahead.

Now freshly showered, it was time to choose her battle dress for the evening. She chose an actual dress, a black thing with spaghetti straps that fit tightly enough to be noticed but not so tightly that it seemed desperate. Its skirt reached down a reasonable distance toward her knees.

Onyx had spent most of the day with her and looked her up and down from her seat on the bed. "Very pretty."

"I am, thank you."

"I meant the dress."

Billie sat at the table and started opening the cases that held her cosmetics. "I know what you meant."

"Should I come along as a chaperone? I'm sure Owen would enjoy talking to me."

She chuckled as she applied eyeliner. "Yeah, that's just what I want, a pixie distracting my date. No thanks." She finished her makeup routine without further comment from Onyx and judged it adequate in the mirror, then pulled open the drawers that held her jewelry. She added several earrings to each ear, a couple of bracelets to each wrist, and one of her favorite necklaces.

Onyx observed, "You wear a lot of jewelry."

"I don't have fancy belts like you do. But if you'd like to borrow some, you can."

Billie touched up her hair as Onyx rooted through the drawers, finally selecting some shiny bracelets and a silver pendant on a soft leather cord.

The pixie asked, "Are these valuable?"

Billie smiled. "Only to me. And I'd love for you to borrow them."

The pixie grinned as she put them on and admired herself in the mirror. "They look better on me."

"I'm sure they do." Billie stood, crossed to her closet, and used a foot to pull out a pair of heels that she stepped into. Then she reached up and pulled down a sparkly black clutch purse that offset the rest of the outfit well.

Onyx commented, "That's impractical."

Billie turned to face the pixie. "It has a strap inside if I need to sling it over a shoulder."

"I mean, it's too small for your weapons."

A chuckle escaped her at the practical observation. "Well, if I want to put anything else in there with it, I suppose you're right. But I am a magical, you know. I probably don't need to carry a gun all the time."

"You could get a thigh holster."

"Those are only real in the movies. For reasonable-sized guns, anyway. I suppose I could put a knife there."

The pixie's voice turned sly. "I'm sure Owen would find that attractive."

Billie laughed. "I don't think Owen will get to see my thigh or my weapons tonight."

"Boring for him."

"Are all pixies as rude as you?"

Onyx clapped happily. "No. I'm special."

Billie raised an eyebrow. "That's just the word for it." Her gaze shifted to Dorian, who was still in his combat knife size, hanging on a hook by the door. "I suppose I could change Dorian's size so he'd fit in the purse. But it would cost me a lot of power and energy to do it, and I don't want to go out physically or magically tired."

"Will you get better at that with practice?"

"I don't know, but that's a good question. Something to figure out. But tonight, I think Dorian will stay home." Billie hugged Onyx goodbye, then portaled to a spot about a block away from the waterfront restaurant where she was meeting Owen. She stared around at the area as she walked, remembering the first fight she'd been part of in DC.

Buildings she'd seen demolished by the giant crab were in the process of reconstruction while others had been leveled and replaced by other things going up in their place. She found Owen right where he was supposed to be, and they exchanged an awkward hug.

"You look beautiful."

She replied, "So do you." And he did. His athletic form fit perfectly into the black jeans, white button-down, and gray jacket, and his sandy hair was a touch disheveled, perfect for running one's fingers through.

He laughed. "I'm secure enough in my masculinity to accept this compliment."

"Good boy," she teased.

He laughed again, then gestured at the waterfront. "It used to look different. I'm sure you've heard about the giant crab attack."

Billie allowed a small smile. "I'm aware of it."

He was almost bouncing as he urged, "Let's go inside. I really think you'll like the place." They headed up one of the long switchback-filled flights of stairs that led to the upper part of the waterfront where all the fancy stuff was. He led her into a restaurant called Radiance, and she immediately felt underdressed. Men in tuxedos and women in gowns dined, accompanied by a string quartet playing in one corner.

Owen must have noticed her reaction, because he chuckled. "Don't worry. We're not eating up here with the fancy folks." He gestured toward a staircase and led the way.

As they descended, she replied, "Thank goodness. I don't know what they're paying you, but I don't think I could have afforded a glass of water in that spot."

"Yeah, it's definitely territory in which we don't belong. Although I kind of hoped you'd be secretly rich."

Billie laughed. "No luck there."

"Curses, foiled again."

The staircase ended in a room about half the size of the one above, which had been expansive. Three bars were in more or less a triangle with seating in between them. Windows looked out on the water. The whole place was brass and stone, and still struck her as a little fancy.

She observed, "Definitely better."

He took her hand gently, laced his fingers through hers, and pulled her toward a hallway. "But not best, yet."

They passed under a sign pointing to the restrooms, and she started to wonder if he, like Onyx, thought he would get to see things that were covered this evening.

He stopped at a large painting with a plaque beside it that read, Still Life with Three Puppies by Paul Gauguin. "Do you like dogs?"

Billie replied, "Of course."

He nodded. "You'll love this one." He pulled on the side of the painting, which swung open on hinges to reveal a doorway.

Beyond it was a hallway with another door that opened onto a bar that felt like the right place for them to be. Dark fabric covered much of the ceiling except where pipes descended for lighting. Plush semicircular booths surrounded the round room, covering two-thirds of the outer wall, with the other third dedicated to a curved stage.

A swing band with a stand-up bass, piano, drummer, guitar, and a pair of vocalists, one male and one female, occupied it. They wore zoot suits and flapper dresses as if it were the 1920s, and laid down a solid groove. Billie laughed. "I love it. Where are we?"

"The Bloodhound Speakeasy. Their only advertising is word-of-mouth, and you have to know the right passwords when you call for a reservation." Owen sounded satisfied.

"You've been here before?"

"Nope, first time. I found out about it about six months ago but didn't have a good reason to visit."

A man in a suit appropriate for the 1920s bustled up to them, then led them to one of the small tables that filled most of the room, arranged in arcs that mirrored the shape of the stage and marched back toward the back wall, leaving a small oval area for dancing.

Billie expected a menu, but Owen explained, "You have three choices. Carnivore, pescatarian, or vegan. They handle everything else."

Billie thought his eyes sparkled very nicely as he shared yet another surprise. "I'll opt for carnivore tonight, please."

Owen nodded. "The same."

The waiter nodded and stepped away. A moment later, a server appeared with a glass of red wine for each of them.

Owen explained, "The courses each come with a matching drink. It's all very put-together, I'm told."

She sipped her wine, a fantastic merlot, which seemed the right flavor for the place. A haze of smoke would have made it perfectly authentic, although not nearly as enjoyable. A charcuterie course was delivered on a single plate, and their fingers touched now and again as they selected morsels, not entirely by chance on either of their parts.

Owen talked about his childhood, growing up in Kansas of all places, and how he had worked his way up through the police academy and made it to the FBI thanks to some strings pulled by one of his senators. He said he loved his work and couldn't imagine doing anything else.

As they finished their salads, which had perfect blue cheese dressing and crumbled blue cheese atop it, Billie shared her background. It included martial arts training and competitions throughout her youth and teens, then her university time studying magic, followed by her move into the AET.

He replied, "So you must be pretty good at magic, huh?"

Billie laughed. "You'd think so, but what I learned in school was more theory and history than practical application. Don't get me wrong, I'm good, but had I spent four years in intensive training with a mentor, I'd be less knowledgeable but more effective."

"Do you wish you'd chosen that route?"

"No, I think I'm adequate to most tasks, and the theoretical knowledge has proven valuable on many occasions."

The main course turned out to be surf and turf, with a filet mignon, a medallion of venison, a lobster tail, and some perfectly seared scallops. Different wines had appeared with each course, all delicious, and another came with dessert, a thin flute of ice wine to complement their carrot cake.

Their conversation turned to some of the challenging things about Owen's job as part of the investigation division. "Probably the hardest part is that we're ultimately cops, so we're busy building cases for court. You have to stay rigorously inside the lines, which can be a challenge when things are complicated or emergent."

Billie frowned. "I've never really faced that, and I'm not sure I do now, actually. So far, we've been very responsive rather than investigative."

"Emergencies like Crystal Colossi will do that to you."

A groan escaped her. "Please don't use that in the plural. I don't even want to think about dealing with another one. Or worse, more than one at a time."

Owen laughed with her. "You should keep it in mind as you enhance the investigative side of your operation."

Her mouth told him she would, but her mind had gone on a different tangent. *I'm sure there will be times I need to color outside the lines. I don't quite know what to do about that. Izzy will probably be able to help me without being discovered, but beyond that, I better not implicate anyone on my team, or it could be trouble for them down the line.*

Owen broke her reverie by asking, "Do you want to dance?"

They did, and time lost meaning for her as she let herself enjoy the moment. Finally, after a couple of hours and a few more drinks, he escorted her to the street. "I suppose you're going to portal back."

She grinned. "It is a convenient advantage of being a magical."

He gestured at the car that pulled up. "And I have to call a car. How mundane."

Billie laughed, and without thinking about it, stood on her tiptoes to hug him. Their lips met briefly, then they each pulled away.

"Will you come out with me again sometime?"

Billie grinned. "Try to stop me."

Unknown to either of them, Onyx crouched on a rooftop nearby, where she'd been keeping an eye on the place. She grinned. She wanted Billie to be happy, and besides, that kiss would give her all kinds of things to tease her friend about.

CHAPTER THIRTEEN

Billie had spent Sunday enjoyably, going for a run, finding a local gym with a pool to do slow laps in, and generally relaxing.

Monday morning had arrived, and it was time for the weekly division heads' meeting. She had chosen a simple business suit but added some extra jewelry because she would see Owen. She got to the room early and discovered him waiting there. It was hard to keep the smile off her face, and he struggled with the same thing.

She'd already checked the HR policies and was sure he had, too. Nothing precluded them from dating since they weren't in power positions relative to one another.

Billie introduced her new admin to Owen and pointed him toward where she would sit. Justin took his spot in a chair along the room's outer wall and pulled out a tablet to take notes on. The coffee area today also held donuts, a decision Billie silently applauded. She chose one and delivered another to her admin with his coffee, then took her seat in one of the chairs arranged around the large conference table.

A moment later, Helen bustled in with others following her like ducklings. Billie had to look away from Owen for fear that she would break into laughter at the sight they both considered amusing.

Helen started the meeting as soon as everyone was seated. When it was her turn to speak, Billie discussed wrapping up the Rafferteys. She made a point of thanking Brandon Shale and his team and received a nod from the CIR division head in return. He spoke about the operation when it was his turn, as well.

No one shared anything earth-shattering, and when the meeting broke up, Helen paused to talk to Billie as the room emptied. "Your team's been doing well. Stitched together a couple of solid wins. But don't get overconfident."

Billie nodded. "Not much chance of that. I have my team members to keep me humble. And they do so. Aggressively."

The corner of Helen's mouth quirked up. "Caleb's good at that."

"They're all good at that," Billie corrected.

Helen laughed. "I guess that's true. In any case, though, they can't all be wins. So, maintain your discipline so you can limit any future damage."

"You got it, boss."

The rest of the morning was spent with paperwork. Billie and Justin worked together to shift most of that burden to him and leave her with the stuff only she could do. She skipped lunch, preferring to continue clearing things off her desk, and was thinking about taking a break when Izzy stepped in.

"We have an appointment with my guy."

Billie looked up. "When?"

"Half an hour."

"How far away is he?"

The infomancer grinned. "Half an hour."

Billie shook her head. "You do this deliberately, don't you?"

Onyx's voice rang out behind Billie. "Of course she does. But it's out of love."

Billie rose, grabbed her jacket from the back of the chair, and shrugged into it. "Maybe offer a little less love in the future."

Eileen and Anya were waiting in the upper level, and the five of them headed for the garage and the SUV inside. The path took her to a part of the city she hadn't visited in person yet. They pulled up outside an unmarked doorway in a long row of industrial-looking storefronts.

Walking through the door revealed the inside was nothing like the outside. While the latter was nondescript, one more doorway in a string of them, the interior was glorious. The floor was wooden planks, obviously aged, but polished to a high sheen. The walls were soft white. Incandescent lighting directed at certain spots filled the ceiling. One had only to follow the beams of those lights to see what was important.

Mannequins along the walls supported armor in various stages of construction with workbenches in between them. Weapon stands were interspersed among the mannequins, and pedestals here and there displayed equipment, some of which was not immediately obvious as to function. Soft music played, and despite the actual largeness of the room and the light colors of the walls that made it seem even bigger, the overall effect was that you had stepped into a comfortable den.

A man walked up to them with a smile. He was in his fifties, she guessed, a shade over five feet tall, and wore weathered jeans and a button-down shirt. An elaborate device perched on his head appeared to be a set of goggles with various lenses that could be snapped in for additional magnification. A tool belt around his waist was full of implements. A gray mustache curled up above his lip, and a matching beard covered his jawline and came to a point at his chin.

He opened his arms wide, and Izzy met him in a big hug. The infomancer lifted him off his feet, and he laughed as she set him down. "I hate it when you do that."

"You've never been a good liar, Jens. You love it." Izzy turned and gestured. "These are my friends. Eileen, Anya, Onyx, and Billie."

He nodded as she pointed each person out. "I'm Jens Brink. Izzy tells me one of you is in need of some custom work."

Anya stepped forward. "It's me. I need something stealth- and infiltration-specific." She gestured around at the items. "Your place is amazing. How many people work here?"

His gaze flicked to Izzy as another smile broke out on his face, then back to Anya. "Only me."

Billie replied, "Really? You do all this yourself?" Not just the quantity of items but the variety made it seem impossible.

"I do. Most of it I do here, in the space you're looking at, but I have a metalworks out back, as well."

"So, you must not have many clients at a time."

His grin widened. "Several."

She frowned in confusion, and he laughed.

Izzy chuckled. "He does this with everyone. Quit fooling around, Jens."

The artisan nodded. "I have a touch of magic that allows me to sleep less and work faster. That's how I manage it. Plus, the work is my passion, so spending a lot of time at it is a pleasure rather than a burden."

Billie felt the truth in his words and, for a moment, wondered why he seemed so convincing.

He looked at Anya. "All right, an infiltration suit. What do you want to include?"

The two went back and forth for a while, discussing possibilities. Then he took them to a drafting table set in a corner. He pulled out a large sheet of paper with a basic human figure on it, a front view on the far left of the page, a back view on the far right, and side views in between.

Jens began to sketch, and Billie saw that he seemed to be working faster than normal. Not super speed, but as if each stroke took less than half as long as it would have normally, and each line was perfect, without any need for thought or adjustment.

He spoke as he worked. "I'll use leather with metal augments. That will reduce the weight and help with sound suppression. The base layer will be ballistic fabric." He looked up for a moment. "Black, I presume?"

Anya nodded. "Yes, definitely."

"All right, its neutral state will be black. It will have armor plates inside,. and I'll strike a balance between protection and mobility, but always with an eye to noise control. I'll thread electronics through it with connection points so you can add items later as needed." He looked at Izzy. "Base unit at the back?"

The infomancer nodded. "That's standard for us, yeah."

"Send me the size."

"Will do."

He went back to sketching. "All right, the plates will be good against bullets, but the fabric won't be. Pretty standard. The outfit will be fairly quiet on its own, but we'll add a unit that detects sounds and phase cancels them with an exact opposite noise. That will still be a sound, but it will be unfamiliar and probably lost in the background."

Anya replied, "That's perfect. I love that."

"It's not a complicated item, but for some reason it hasn't caught on with military or AET yet. I guess they don't really have a need for stealth."

Eileen asked, "Heat detection?"

"The suit will match the surrounding temperature. There's an insulating layer inside the fabric that will keep the wearer cool or warm, but it draws power, as do other elements of the suit, so you'll have to be careful when using it." He tapped the end of his pencil against his teeth as he looked up at the ceiling. "Another thing that draws power, but you might want, is chameleon fabric."

Izzy replied, "She'll definitely want chameleon fabric."

Eileen added, "If she doesn't, I do."

Anya asked, "Is that what it sounds like?"

"It is. Tiny lenses survey the environment, and an electronic skin on the fabric changes to match it. It's not perfect, but it's good."

Billie observed, "That would be useful to have when magic isn't an option."

Anya agreed. "Let's do it."

Onyx whispered to Billie, "I need that."

Billie replied, "Why?"

"So I can sneak around the office and surprise people."

"No." Billie interrupted her follow-up protest with, "Shhh."

Eileen asked, "Is there a way to increase the suit's power?"

Jens lifted a shoulder. "More batteries, but it adds weight."

"Will you share the schematics of your batteries?"

"They're off the shelf. Happy to."

"Maybe we can improve on that part and deliver more power with the same weight."

Jens added, "I can include an internal harness system attached to a line launcher, here." He sketched a tube on the figure's left forearm. "We can put a magnetic and/or a harpoon on it, plus a small motor. Useful for infiltration when you have to climb."

Anya nodded. "Sounds great. Can you do anything with the gloves to make climbing easier?"

"I can make them grippy, that's easy enough. I could add extendable spikes to the toes and the fingers, but that takes power, adds weight, and isn't particularly surreptitious."

"The harpoon will be fine."

Jens sketched out a few more things, then he, Izzy, and Eileen discussed interfacing the lenses in the mask with their comm system. They also discussed incorporating additional sensing systems. After an hour's work, they were done.

Billie asked, "How long to deliver?"

"A couple of days."

"That fast?"

He grinned. "I love my work."

Anya clapped. "All right. Now we're really ready to go, or will be in a couple of days."

CHAPTER FOURTEEN

When Billie got to the office on Tuesday morning, she was surprised to see the light on her desk phone blinking. Most people who wanted to get in touch with her called her cell phone. She played back the message and discovered it was from Brandon Shale, inviting her out for coffee whenever she got in. *Nice of him not to invade my off-work time with something that could wait.*

She returned his call, and they met at a nearby Starbucks, where she got a flat white with several shots of flavoring. He joined her a moment later with a double espresso in hand. He sipped it, which seemed like a strange affectation for the leader of the Critical Incident Response team, whose members Izzy had described as possessing an overwhelming amount of testosterone.

They chatted a little about the adventure they had shared going after Raffertey, then he divulged, "I have a guy who wants to jump divisions, from mine to yours."

"I'm not poaching your people."

"I didn't say you were. It's his call. I've been waiting for him to do something like this for a while."

"All right, as long as you understand that I don't want to steal from you."

"I get it, although if any of your people ever suggest jumping over to my unit, you can be assured I'll say yes in an instant, theft or not."

Billie grinned. "They're pretty good, I can't argue with that."

"Prem will be another solid addition. He's a high flyer who needs new challenges, and he thinks he's gotten all he can from my unit. Frankly, I agree."

"What does he do?"

"I'd rather let him speak for himself. I told him we were meeting, so he's doubtless waiting in his lab to talk to you right now."

Billie laughed. "That's a little evil. For him and me. Putting us on the spot."

He finished his espresso and nonchalantly tossed the cup into a can six feet away, sinking the shot perfectly. "Yeah, I'm a jerk like that."

They walked back to headquarters together, and Brandon delivered her to Prem's lab. As he left, she mused that he was constantly surprising her and that she liked him more than she'd thought she would. *Probably a good thing if events keep combining our teams.*

Billie took in the lab, which was outfitted with microscopes, computers, and other things that hit her senses as being biological in nature. Prem was seated on a high stool, staring at her. He was an inch or so taller than her, with an average build, dark eyes, and shortish black hair. He wore khakis and an ironed polo shirt.

She apologized, "Sorry, thinking shallow thoughts very intently. I'm Billie Keller." She went over and extended a hand.

He stood and took it. "Prem Patel."

"Brandon says you're interested in switching over to my team."

He nodded. "I thought CIR would be educational for me, and it has been. I've definitely improved my abilities in trauma medicine. But I haven't been able to use my investigation skills, which aren't limited to medicine."

Billie tilted her head. "You're a doctor?"

He raised a hand and wiggled it. "Somewhere between an EMT and a doctor. I finished my courses but haven't done my residency. I chose this instead, for the moment. I made sure I can step back in where I left off, and plan to finish and be an official MD at some point."

"Of course. After all that work, it would be crazy not to. What roles do you want to fill on my team?"

"I've been a field medic for the CIR, so I can fill that role easily. I can do most forensic work. I'm good at talking to people, and I fit in most places pretty well. I can talk science to scientists, and sports to sports executives."

"That's an interesting mix of talents."

He smiled, and it transformed him from average to handsome. "I like to think so."

"We have several nonmagicals on the team, and having a medic would be good for that. We've been carrying around basic first aid and trauma kits, but this would be better. Can you fight?"

He crossed his arms, and Billie's brain checked off that this was an issue for him. "I can shoot. I'm qualified with pistol and rifle. I have to be for CIR. But I prefer carrying stun weapons and nonlethal equipment."

Billie nodded. "Doctor stuff."

"Yeah."

The decision was an easy one. "All right, let's give it a try."

His body language softened. "All right."

"Come on, you can choose your office." They walked back through CIR and across the hall to Magical Threats. He selected a lab. Caleb joined them, introduced himself, then looked at Billie. "Our new demolitions expert will be here tomorrow."

She grinned. "All right. Full complement."

"And nothing to do."

"Well, get busy finding us some work."

He laughed. "Sure, I'll just go whip up a magical threat."

"Perfect. Get to it."

Billie finished chatting with Prem, introduced him to Justin, and set the pair on the path to completing the paperwork for Prem's transfer. Her desk phone rang, and Helen requested, "Can you come upstairs, please?"

Billie replied, "Of course. Private meeting?"

"No. You can bring others if you like."

Billie rounded up Caleb and Onyx and took the elevator upstairs to the top floor. Inside Helen's large office were three people, including her boss and one non-human. Billie's eyes widened at the sight of the small dragon with butterfly wings. She recognized Arthur Blackwood, but he stood and reintroduced himself anyway.

Then he added, "These are two of my stars from Spell-bound Security's Cleveland office, Danica Grey and her companion, Jilly."

Danica extended her hand. "Helen's been telling us about your unit, Billie. Sounds good." The other woman wore a tailored business suit in dark blue and had notably red lipstick and nail polish. A few pieces of jewelry flashed in the light as they shook.

"You can't trust her. She's biased."

Movement caught Billie's attention as the colorful dragon flew in a circle around Onyx before landing on the pixie's shoulder. Her multi-hued scales glimmered in the sunlight that came through the windows.

The dragon asked in a high, playful voice, "What are you?"

Onyx replied, "Less rude than you, apparently."

Jilly snorted. "I'm a fae dragon. You're not a human. What are you?"

"I'm a pixie."

The dragon leapt off her shoulder and hovered in front to look at her. Her butterfly wings beat quickly to keep her in position. "You're a little big for a pixie."

"You're a little small for a dragon. And I can change my size."

Jilly flew in a small loop, and happy laughter escaped her. "So can I. Do you think we're related?"

Laughter burst out of Onyx, and Billie realized she'd been holding it back, pretending to be irritated. "No, I don't think so, but I wish we were."

She sat, and Jilly landed on her shoulder again. "Me too. Can we say we're related?"

"Absolutely. I'd love to call you my sister."

Jilly told Danica, "I have a sister now."

Danica rolled her eyes as she retook her seat. "Of course you do." The other woman's gaze landed on Billie. "Jilly's very friendly."

"I see that."

Jilly continued to pepper Onyx with questions, and Onyx's whispered replies caused the dragon to whisper as well.

Arthur interjected, "Danica has a project going on you might want to be a part of."

Danica explained, "Our infomancer made a run the other night that got us some data we've finally decrypted. It seems that the group targeting our client is a larger organization than we'd expected."

Arthur added, "Of course, I could have brought in other Spellbound offices to assist, but it seemed like a great chance to get your unit involved with my people."

Helen countered, "A great chance to shift some of the cost to the federal government, you mean."

Arthur waved off her comment. "Potato, po-tah-toe."

Everyone laughed at that.

Helen looked at Billie. "I think it's a valuable opportunity unless you have something else on your plate. Part of the vision for Magical Threats was always that it would interact with other organizations that do similar work."

Billie replied, "I wish we were busier, but we're still working the connection that Izzy found in Raffertey's records. It looks like it might never amount to anything. So, we're good. Let's do it." She addressed Danica. "What did you have in mind?"

"We've located what might be the enemy's base. We have some remote surveillance on it now, but they have a lot of cameras on the exterior, and we can't get too close. And they must be using portals for transport since there's no one going in or out. Thermals show a large number of people inside at all times of the day."

Caleb nodded. "Logical assumption. All magicals? Mixed group?"

"No idea."

Billie replied, "All right. It sounds like something we can help with."

Caleb added, "We should probably operate as separate units if we're doing this soon, or do we have enough time to practice together enough to work as one?"

Danica replied, "We're looking at tomorrow night."

"Okay then, separate units it is."

Billie suggested, "Our infomancer can work with yours to coordinate efforts ahead of time and during the mission, if that's cool with you."

Danica nodded. "Sounds good."

Jilly interjected, "We're the best."

Onyx countered, "We're pretty good."

Jilly replied decisively, "Then you're the best, too."

They talked for a while longer, and as they separated, Danica pulled Billie aside. The other woman remarked, "The higher-ups' agenda notwithstanding, I've heard about your successes so far. I'm glad to be working with you."

Billie replied, "Arthur speaks well of you, too. The same."

When they were back in the hallway of their own area,

Billie commented, "Just when I think I know what this job is, it takes a turn."

Caleb laughed. "It's like being in the rapids. You've just got to go with it and keep your head above water."

Onyx replied, "Doggy paddle for life."

Caleb tilted his head. "I wonder if we could trade Onyx for Jilly?"

The pixie returned a thin-lipped smile. "I wonder how you'd like to wake up in the embrace of a cocoon of poison ivy."

Caleb raised a hand. "Forget I said anything."

The pixie looked smug. "Thought so."

As Caleb walked away, he called back to Billie, "Control your child."

Billie laughed. "Onyx is uncontrollable now. I can't imagine what she was like as a toddler."

The pixie laughed. "I was the best. Ask Jilly."

CHAPTER FIFTEEN

The next evening, Billie followed Anya into the arming room. She sat on a bench while the other woman opened her locker and drew out her new armor, which had been delivered earlier that day. She held it up. "This is going to look good."

Billie laughed. "No one's going to see how good it looks if everything goes right, at least until after the mission."

"You might not be thinking this all the way through. I'm not planning on taking down everyone inside myself, you know." She began to don the armor, first stepping into the flexible fabric and pulling it up her legs.

"Damn. What's the use of you, then?"

Anya started to fasten the suit's connectors. "I like the feel of this."

"You've been crazy excited for that thing since the moment we walked into that dude's workshop. You'd pretend to love it even if it weren't awesome."

"Accurate. But I'm not pretending." Anya activated the

suit's systems and grunted as it sealed itself up around her. "Tight."

"You wanted freedom of motion, you've got freedom of motion."

"If I gain a pound, I'm going to have to take it in for alterations."

She laughed at her scout. "That's why we have a gym."

Anya raised her arm and sighted down it. The small arrowhead of the harpoon, which would stab into or magnetically adhere to a surface or expand out into a hook depending on the need of the moment, glimmered under the overhead lights. "I hope this thing does everything he said it will."

"Izzy believes in him. Arguably she's smart enough to trust."

Anya tucked her hair in as she pulled the mask up over her head and it automatically sealed to the rest of the suit. The lenses over her eyes were dark and only slightly shinier than the rest of the outfit. Billie heard Anya's words over the comm unit in her ear, rather than out loud, as the mask and suit eliminated the sound. "Comm check."

Ensconced behind her computers in her office, Izzy replied, "Comm check successful. Can you hear me?"

Anya replied, "Affirmative."

"Good. Seems like the comm system integrates perfectly. I can access all your suit sensors, and I think they'll make Eileen jealous."

Anya laughed. "She already asked me if she can deconstruct the suit to reverse-engineer it. I told her to buy her own and leave mine alone."

"Rude, but a good choice."

"I thought so."

"Hang on, I'll loop us in with the Spellbound team." Izzy hit some buttons, and a small ding sounded in her ear as a new communication channel was established. "This is Z, from Magical Threats."

A familiar voice replied, "Voltaic, from Spellbound. Hang on while I get you synced up."

Izzy chuckled. Her voice was different when she used either of her online avatars, so there was no reason for Voltaic to connect the person speaking with her to her friend on the web, Alloy. Voltaic sounded the same as she always did, so she couldn't help teasing the other woman. "I hear you and your team are pretty good."

Voltaic replied, "They're not bad. I'm excellent, of course."

The humor came through, and Izzy laughed. "Of course. You're the best, according to what the dragon said."

"*Fae* dragon. She's very insistent on the full naming."

Izzy chuckled again. "I stand corrected. The fae dragon."

"She bites, so it's good to stay on her friendly side." A moment later, new voices sounded in the background and Voltaic reported, "You're looped in. You'll hear our channel at a lower volume unless my AI senses it's directed at you or unless you instruct the AI to include you fully."

"Good deal. Looking forward to working with you." *Again.*

"Same, same."

Anya commented, "Seems like everything's a go."

Billie replied, "All right. Let's head up to the lobby."

Anya spoke to the security guard, and he deactivated the anti-magic field that protected the lobby. A portal opened with Spellbound folks on the opposite side, and Billie and Anya stepped through.

Billie introduced, "Anya, this is Danica, and that's Jilly."

Anya grinned at the dragon, whom she had only heard about secondhand. "Pleased to meet you both."

Jilly replied enthusiastically, "And you. I love making new friends."

Danica chuckled. "Anya, this is Alexandra, my second-in-command. She'll be going with you tonight." Anya shook hands with the other woman, who was a little bigger than her but otherwise had a similar build. Scouts often did.

Danica asked, "We're good to go?"

Alex replied, "I am."

Anya added, "Same here."

Danica nodded. "Let's do it then." She opened another portal that led to an empty street. They crossed over, and Voltaic fed a map into Anya's display, and presumably Alex's as well. It showed their location relative to the enemy's presumed base, which was a block away.

Anya reported, "Looks good," and Alex agreed.

"All right, we'll go get ready to back you up." Billie

opened a portal and stepped back into the lobby of the headquarters building.

Danica stepped back through her own portal. "Same here. Stay in touch." The rift closed, leaving the two scouts alone.

Anya commented, "All right, let's see what these jerks are up to." She cast a veil around both of them, having been informed ahead of time that Alexandra wasn't a magical. They stayed against the wall of the nearest building as they approached their target, then crossed the street in the dark space between overhead lights. The precaution was probably unnecessary given the protection of her magic invisibility, but good practices plus magic were always better than either alone.

The building was two stories high, and on their map it looked square. Voltaic advised, "This used to be a corporate building. I'm not sure what it was used for, but it was neither a headquarters nor a warehouse according to what I've been able to dig up. No idea what the inside will look like. It's been vacant for a while, supposedly."

Anya replied, "Sure looks it." The building had once had plentiful windows on the ground floor, but now it had plywood instead. The doors she could see were chained shut, and the rust on the chain suggested it had been there for a while.

They advanced toward the building until Voltaic snapped, "Stop."

Anya recognized Z's voice as her team's infomancer asked, "What do you have?"

"Cameras, for sure. More of them than this kind of building would normally have."

Izzy replied, "And concealed fairly well, to boot. Yeah, that's notable."

Voltaic instructed, "Alex, deploy Robin."

Alex reached for her belt, opened a pouch, and lifted out a small rectangular piece of plastic and metal. Anya watched it unfold until it resembled a bird, but not a robin.

She remarked on that, and Alex replied, "Voltaic thinks she's funny. She gives it a different bird name every time. Apparently, her actual job isn't interesting or exciting enough for her, so she has to make it weirder for everyone." She tossed it in the air, and its wings flapped as it flew away, looking exactly like a real bird.

Anya commented, "We need one of those."

Izzy replied, "Agreed. It's a brilliant idea. Eileen will be ticked since we just made our own mini drone that doesn't look like a bird." She laughed. "I can't wait to tell her."

Anya's display filled with information as the drone flew near the building, and she recognized the symbols for motion sensors, sound detectors, and heat registers. Worst of all, the icon representing magic sensors popped up in sufficient quantity that she was sure their target had created a field to cover the whole building. She muttered, "Definitely not abandoned, then."

Izzy replied, "Give us a minute."

On a channel to only Voltaic, Izzy stated, "I'll go into the system. You stay out here and coordinate activities."

She got the reply she'd expected. "How about we do it the other way around?"

Izzy laughed. "Roll for it?"

"Cool."

Given infomancers' abilities to cheat at almost anything, a site had cropped up that was hack-proof and simple to allow for decision-making. The players selected a number of dice and the system rolled them. In this case, they chose six six-sided dice. Voltaic needled, "I rolled a twenty-four. Beat that."

Izzy triggered her roll and watched as the dice fell into place. "I got twenty-seven. Sorry." She added playfully, "Loser."

Voltaic laughed. "Rude. Next one's mine."

"Fair." Izzy sent a message to the Magical Threats team to let them know she'd be out of contact for a bit and shifted her awareness fully into her computers. Nakano's dressing room appeared around her, and she quickly moved to the technological portion, disregarding the Japanese temple replica that held her normal armor. A capsule in the corner held her stealth gear, a black set of samurai armor with black cloth clothing over it filled with pockets containing useful items. A different katana, this one matte black metal, accompanied it.

When she was fully armed and armored, she headed out into the magical dark web. Voltaic had already located the server address for this location, and when Nakano landed there, she discovered the server looked like the building. "Lazy, unimaginative, and boring. But hopefully the security is as stupid as the design." The structure had cameras positioned around the outside in the same locations as in the physical world.

Nakano reached into her belt and retrieved a handful of

small spheres that looked vaguely like tiny BBs. She flicked them away one after the next, and they flew unerringly to stick to each camera. They would cause the image to loop and allow her to approach unseen. Fortunately, her analysis tools told her that was the only defensive measure the virtual building shared with the physical one. She walked the building's perimeter until she found an exhaust vent for the HVAC system, pulled a small tool kit from her gauntlet, loosened the screws, and set the grate aside.

Nakano climbed in, pulled the vent cover back into place, and used adhesive magnets to secure it. The exhaust tube narrowed to an uncomfortable tightness as she moved through it, which left her using mainly her fingers and toes to scrabble forward. The rest of her body was unable to do much more than wriggle like a snake. Fortunately, she found her destination before the claustrophobia really kicked in.

Beyond the grate of an air vent was a security room with a single uniformed guard who leaned back in his chair with his feet up on the desk. He might have been asleep, but she couldn't tell from her angle. *If he isn't, he soon will be.*

She maneuvered her hand and arm to reach into another pouch and pulled out more small spheres. These were plain white and fit easily through the ridges on the vent after she transferred them to her other hand. When they hit the floor, translucent vapor puffed out. Her aim was perfect, and the fog engulfed the security guard. His head drooped, and his body went limp.

Nakano pried the vent cover away and let herself down into the room, then moved to the single door and rammed wedges into the openings to keep it secured. She tapped on some keyboards and activated her comm. "The magic detector is down. I'm leaving the others up so my infiltration is less likely to be noticed."

After Izzy finished talking, Voltaic advised the stealth duo, "You're good to go, just keep that magic veil going."

Anya replied, "Affirmative," and moved closer to the building with Alex at her side. She created blocks of force magic to form stairs that they walked up to the roof.

Voltaic reported, "The bird showed several turbine fans on the top. I think they're probably for exhaust. You should be able to jam them if needed to get a look below."

"Got it."

As soon as they reached the top, Alex whispered, "I'll go across."

Anya replied, "Good deal, I'll stay on this side." She focused part of her mind on keeping her ally shrouded and applied another part to use force magic to stop the fan from spinning. Luckily, it wasn't electrical but moved by wind power. She dropped a fiber-optic camera line down from inside her sleeve and guided it through the attached air system with force magic. The first vent she found showed a large room with maybe a half-dozen people seated around the table eating.

She pulled the camera back, moved it in a different direction, and located a single room with someone cleaning a weapon. The third vent she had access to showed an empty room. Alex reported similar results.

Anya remarked, "Well, there are definitely people in there, boss, but I'm afraid we don't have much to offer about them from up here."

Billie replied, "All right. Figure out the best spot for us to breach from the roof. Danica says her team will go in from the ground. We'll be there shortly."

CHAPTER SIXTEEN

Billie marched into the equipping room with Caleb and Onyx at her heels. The others were already present since they had been loitering nearby when word came down to move. She headed to her locker and pulled out her armor, then checked to ensure their newest members, Hannah and Prem, were both finding their equipment properly. It was the first time her team would roll out in its full version, and she wished it had been a little less haphazard.

Caleb probably read her expression. "Don't sweat it, boss. We got this. And hell, we have help. Gotta love that."

Onyx observed, "I'm guessing Jilly is a real wild card."

Caleb snorted. "Like you're not."

She smiled. "So says the person who desperately needs a club to the head."

As she slid on her base layer with most of her armor pieces already in place, Billie replied, "Settle down, you two. No braining each other before a mission. You want to fight, I'll set that up."

Onyx replied, "Bring it."

Caleb laughed. "Don't you already have a match against Anya to deliver on?"

"Both of you at once."

Caleb laughed again. "We'll discuss it after."

Billie tossed a package to Onyx. "If you're not going to wear armor, you at least have to wear this harness."

"Maybe I should get some fancy armor like Anya's."

"Maybe you should. Do pixies have money?"

"Not really, but I'm sure I could steal whatever I needed."

Billie shook her head. "Why is it that every member of this team goes right to criminality? First Izzy, now you." She fastened her uniform, then pulled out additional armor pieces to slide into several of the slots. It was the kind of night where it felt like more armor would be better.

She was still amazed by how well the small rectangular pieces of metal clicked together and how well they moved. After the visit to the custom armor maker, Eileen's competitive nature would probably have her working hard on new and interesting innovations of her own, which would be good for the team.

Billie closed her locker when she was fully armored except for the helmet she carried.

Onyx asked, "Is this good?" The pixie had a harness around her torso that would allow her to drop with the rest of them.

Billie replied, "Looks good."

Voltaic spoke over the comm. "Basher, Z requests you bring a drone. We'll have some too."

"Got it." She turned to Hannah. "You and Prem grab one of the drone cases from the other room once you're geared up, please."

She nodded. "Got it, boss."

As Billie followed Prem into the weapons room, she noted he had a custom backpack she hadn't seen before. Doubtless it was filled with his medical gear, as were the pouches on the fronts and backs of his upper legs. The sight made her feel good. Her hand strayed unconsciously to tap the spot on her belt where her potions resided and ensure the flasks were still in their containers.

Billie selected a rifle and adjusted the strap until it hung where she wanted it. A pistol belt went on next, and she clipped Dorian's sheath onto that, then slid extra magazines into their holders on the armor.

Beside her, Hannah selected a shotgun, mirroring Caleb. It figured that their demolitions expert would want something that made a louder bang. Prem held a stun rifle that he must have brought from Critical Incident Response since she hadn't had the foresight to get him one here. That was something for Justin to handle later.

As Billie stared at the grenade options, Prem approached her. She reached up into a cabinet, pulled out four healing potions from their backup supply, and handed them to him. "In case our magicals are down and can't drink it themselves."

He slid them into the same type of containers on his belt that she had on hers. "I already had one, but this will help. Thanks."

Billie went back to selecting her grenades. She wasn't sure what they would face or how dangerous they would be, but she decided to opt for nonlethal. Their new demolitions expert would handle anything that needed to be blown up, so she had the latitude to carry incapacitating grenades rather than injury-causing. She selected one each of gas, lightning, and flash-bang grenades, then added a fragmentation option as a last resort choice, hoping she wouldn't have cause to use it.

Billie opened a portal, cast a veil over her team, and closed it when everyone had passed through, including the drone they were bringing along. She maintained the veil as they moved down the street and was impressed at how close Voltaic kept the drone to them. When they reached the building, they climbed up the same way the scouts had. Anya appeared as Billie's veil covered her and pointed at a part of the roof.

Billie instructed, "Bomber, have at it."

Hannah replied, "On it." She set charges in a circle centered upon the point Anya had indicated, each of which blinked with a green light to indicate its readiness.

Billie moved to a nearby piece of HVAC equipment and attached a super-strong electromagnet to it as Caleb did the same on another unit, still protected by her veil. Her team attached their lines to them, then readied themselves to move.

Billie asked, "Everyone good to go?" Affirmatives came back. "Voltaic?"

The Spellbound infomancer replied, "Stand by. Merging channels." A moment later, they heard Danica's voice as she verified her team was ready as well. Then Danica asked, "Basher, you ready to go?"

"You know it."

The other woman ordered, "Voltaic, countdown from fifteen."

A countdown appeared in her display, and Billie grinned at Caleb. "First run for the full team."

He looked up toward the heavens. "Why do you mention these things before a mission? Are you *trying* to curse us?"

"Because I love that it makes you uncomfortable."

"You're not nice."

Hannah setting off the charges ended the conversation. The debris all went down. Billie had been confident it would, based on how controlled the demolitions expert's work had been on the movie set. She ran forward with Onyx at her side and jumped into the hole behind the drone, which buzzed down ahead of her.

CHAPTER SEVENTEEN

The drone zipped away through an open door as Billie's boots hit the floor with Onyx right beside her. She had dropped ready to fight with her rifle in her hands, which was lucky given the three enemies that were present who hadn't been in the room during the recon and were bringing pistols up. She aimed at the nearest and pulled the trigger, delivering a three-round burst that struck him in the shoulder, spun him around, and slammed him into the wall. He rebounded and fell, doing nothing to deter his fall. She counted him out of the fight.

A spoken word caused the connector at the end of her line to release, and the line retracted into her belt at high speed. It scraped across the armor plate of the arm she brought up to defend against the second man, who had thrown himself at her instead of shooting. She blocked his punch, then used a force blast that should have thrown him into the back corner of the room, and maybe through the wall. Unfortunately, it didn't move him an inch.

Billie snapped, "Magical in here," and charged him. She

pushed magic into her muscles and wrapped her fists and shins in force magic to trade blows with the man, who was larger than she and looked like he worked out.

His strikes weren't powerful enough to get through her shields, but hers, aided by magic, quickly overcame his defenses. A punch connected and broke several of his ribs. He leaned to the side with a groan, and she delivered a roundhouse punch with the other fist that landed on the side of his face, sending him down to join his friend on the floor.

She spun and saw that Onyx was engaged with a third, using her clubs to batter his shield. Billie shouted, "I need some dust."

The pixie threw one of the clubs up toward the hole in the roof, grabbed her belt with her free hand while still striking with the other club, and tossed dust into the air. Billie used a wave of force to send it spiraling through the room, where it outlined the veiled magical in the corner.

If she'd had more time, or fewer likely enemies, she would have chosen differently, but instead grabbed her rifle, pointed it at the corner, and shot three times, low, middle, and high.

The second bullet caught the magical in the chest, and his shield dissipated. He stared at her in shock, and she blasted him with lightning to drop him. A moment after he thumped to the floor, Onyx clubbed her opponent down to join him, then picked up her fallen club from the floor.

Billie commented, "I thought you were going to be fancy and catch that," as she moved toward the doorway out of the room.

Onyx shifted to the opposite side of the door and

grabbed the handle. "I'm cool, but not *that* cool, unfortunately."

The comm was littered with people shouting "Contact!" and sharing information. Billie held up three fingers, then two, then one, and Onyx yanked the door open. She dashed through it with her rifle ready and ended up in a large central corridor. When she saw the stairs at the far end, her mind finally put together the fact that this portion of the building had two actual floors, and she was on the upper one.

As she veiled herself and moved down the hallway, the nauseatingly familiar feel of her magic vanishing hit her. She snapped, "Z, turn off that anti-magic emitter."

The infomancer replied, "There's no control for it here. I'll try to find it."

***

Onyx had followed Billie into the hallway and was a few feet behind her as the other woman ran toward the stairs at the far end. A moment later, seemingly without transition, Onyx was flying backward down the hallway with a sharp pain in her chest. She put the pieces together mid-flight. Her chest hurt because she'd been punched. The being who had punched her was a seven-foot-tall Kilomea that was ogre-ish in appearance and scowling, and was marching down the hallway toward her.

Her back hit the floor, and she forced herself into a backward somersault to reach her feet. A snarl escaped her as she flipped her clubs in her hands. Pixies and Kilomea as overall groups had an unpredictable relationship. Sometimes they were buddy-buddy. Other times they reacted to each other in a less positive way, which often involved fighting. He had punched her because he was a bad guy, not because he was a Kilomea, but it still put their relationship into the negative column.

Onyx rushed at him, not content to stand still and let him hammer her with the momentum he'd built up. She faked jumping for his head and slid on the floor, going between his legs. His knee slammed down as her head went past, and she chided herself for forgetting that Kilomea were born warriors, both fast and strong. By the time he got turned, she was ready.

She flicked her club at him. "All right, scumbag, let's see what you've got when you aren't attacking by surprise. Kilomea are such dirty fighters."

The taunt was intended to enrage him, and succeeded. He bellowed as he rushed forward and drew his right fist back. She dodged to the side as he threw the punch but hit the wall. She only realized it was a feint when his shoulder slammed into her and knocked her backward again.

Onyx planted her feet against the stumble and counterattacked. Her clubs twisted at the end of each strike to impact the tender spots of the arms he used to block, connecting with his elbows, wrists, and the bones in his forearms. The knobby heads of her clubs struck hard, drawing howls of pain and anger.

It didn't stop him. She retreated steadily as he pressed the attack, waiting for him to take one step that put him even slightly off-balance. She darted back to draw him in, then stopped. He lurched forward, then planted his leg, giving her what she wanted.

She whipped both clubs around in a horizontal strike that slammed into the side of his knee. It buckled, and the Kilomea dropped with a crash.

Onyx reached for her belt, grabbed two studs, and ripped them free. She crushed them in her hand and blew the dust into his face, which screwed up into an expression of dismay as the hot peppers burned the membranes in his nose and eyes. The involuntary heaving as he sneezed drew more of it into his system.

She collected herself, readied her weapons, then jumped up and whacked him in the center of his forehead with both of her clubs. His eyes crossed, and he fell limply to his back. She selected a different dust and blew it into his face. His eyes went dreamy as the hallucinogen hit, and she shook her head at him.

"Stay down, big boy. If you join the fight again, you won't survive it." Then she turned and ran after Billie, intending to offer an important comment about ensuring your partner was okay before you ran willy-nilly into enemy territory.

Anya's drop had delivered her into an empty room on the first level. Her line had stuck when she triggered it to reel in, and it took her several moments to get it properly retracted. She headed to the door, pulled it open from the side, and stuck her head into the opening. Across the hall was an open door with several people visible through it. The one in the front held a machine pistol, and she jerked back as bullets flew past her and slammed into the far wall.

She let her rifle fall as she drew her pistol with one hand and grabbed a grenade with the other. She stuck her hand around the doorframe, pulled the trigger repeatedly, and blindly threw the grenade above head height, hoping it would make it into the room. She stuffed her pistol back in its holster, grabbed her rifle, and ran into the hallway after the grenade went off.

The first man in line was on the floor and bleeding, probably from one of her bullets. Another who had been standing behind him looked stunned, but had a pistol pointed roughly in her direction. That gave her only one option. She pulled the trigger.

Three bullets hit him in the chest, and he staggered backward. She let the rifle drop as she crossed the threshold into the room, put her hands on the man she'd shot, and pushed him into the next closest enemy. A curse burst from her lips as she discovered three more foes were in the room. Fortunately, two of them were still shrugging off the effects of the flash-bang grenade.

Anya went for the third, ducked as he pulled the trigger on his pistol, then spun to deliver a strike to the arm that held it to knock it out of his hand.

She finished her spin with an elbow to the back of his head. He got a hand up to partially block it and rammed a knee into her lower back. She grunted, stepped forward, arched way back and grabbed his neck, then crouched and slammed her body back to lever him over her head. She resisted the urge to add the neck twist that might have made the move fatal.

He screamed, but it cut off as he slammed into the floor hard enough to pass out.

The other two were regaining their wits. Anya delivered a skipping side kick to the knee of the nearest. It crunched, and she kicked him in the head as he went down. The next one blocked her first punch and evaded her second, then tried a low kick. She blocked his shin with her armored one, and he howled in pain.

She grinned. "I notice you're not wearing armor. Bad choice, scumbag." She threw a series of punches at his torso, and each block he used damaged him more. Soon he was on the floor, curled up in the fetal position and struggling to breathe, which meant he was essentially out of the fight. She called, "Where is everybody?"

Billie replied, "We have most of the bad guys down. Come to the middle of the building, bottom floor. We found something weird."

CHAPTER EIGHTEEN

Billie stared into the plunging hole in the floor. Only about ten feet was visible in the room's light before it dwindled into darkness. Low light vision gave her some more, but it was too deep to see the bottom. It was about six feet in radius, much larger than anything had any reason to be in a building like this. Metal ladders were attached to each side. "That's suspicious, weird, and unexpected."

Danica replied, "Good description."

Two drones whipped past and dropped into the hole. Voltaic interjected, "We'll have more information soon."

Jilly interjected, "It's not getting any smaller," and dove in. Danica growled something under her breath, and both she and the rest of the Spellbound team moved to tie off their descent lines.

Billie added, "Guess we're all going down." She attached her line and jumped, careful to control the speed of her descent. Her armor's lights revealed that the perfectly cylindrical tunnel was carved out of the rock and showed no signs of differentiation or wear. She couldn't imagine what kind of machine could accomplish that and guessed it had been done magically.

Voltaic reported, "Tunnel at the bottom goes in two directions."

Billie instructed, "Let's group up before we move on and let the drone scout."

Danica replied, "Agreed. I'm at the bottom. Seems safe."

Billie landed and discovered that it was also beyond the range of the anti-magic emitter. She shielded herself, then ordered her team to apply shields to themselves and their non-magical partners. The drones hovered nearby.

Voltaic requested, "Let me know when you're ready."

Billie checked to ensure everyone was protected, reloaded, and ready to go as Danica did the same for her team.

Danica ordered, "Send the drones."

Windows opened in Billie's display to show the feeds from the drones as they sped off down the hallways. The bright lights happened a minute before the sounds echoed back toward them. She snapped, "What happened?"

Voltaic replied, "Rewinding, slo-mo." The feed from one drone showed two turrets flicking out of the walls and concentrating their fire on the drone, destroying it in an instant. The other drone feed whited out, and Voltaic advised, "Sensors show explosions from both walls on the second one."

Billie asked Danica, "My magicals scout, others rear guard?"

The other woman nodded. "Good plan."

Billie, Onyx, Jilly, and Danica took one tunnel, while

Anya, Caleb, Hannah, and Deacon took the other. The magicals on Danica's team were staying to help with the rear guard. Hannah handed over several heavy satchel charges before shrugging her backpack back on.

Danica asked, "Turrets or explosions?"

Onyx replied, "Turrets, please."

Billie confirmed, "Okay, turrets it is."

They moved cautiously down the hall with Danica and Billie in the lead, side by side. They froze and braced for bullets when the turrets came into view, but none came. "Guess we need to get closer before they're active."

Danica replied, "And we have to get closer before we can do anything to them."

Jilly volunteered, "I'll distract them." She shot off at a speed Billie wouldn't have expected. When the guns opened up, the dragon curled into a tight ball and let her momentum carry her forward.

Billie's eyes widened at the sight of bullets striking the little dragon and changing her trajectory until she realized they weren't penetrating. She dashed forward beside Danica until they were close enough, then both lofted their satchels and used magic to guide them to their destination. Billie triggered them, and both turrets evaporated.

Danica explained, "The impacts hurt Jilly some, but her scales let nothing through. Nothing we've met yet, anyway."

Onyx replied, "So she's the ultimate scout."

"Except for the nonstop talking."

Jilly flew back. "Come on, what are you waiting for?" She hurtled back down the tunnel.

Billie quipped, "She told us."

Danica replied, "She always does. Let's move."

Anya moved cautiously down the hallway, pausing between each step to allow her suit's sensors to scan for danger. If she'd been designing the defenses for this type of place, she would have ensured the drone made it past several other traps before destroying it to catch followers unaware.

Voltaic warned, "I've got explosives in the walls ahead of you, plus there are a lot of frequencies around that could be detectors. I don't recognize the signals, but I wouldn't trust them, either. Hell, they might have a camera and someone with a finger on a button."

Anya replied, "Affirmative." To the others, she added, "Let's create force shields around ourselves and inside the tunnel. Give me two feet away from the walls and ceilings. Double them up."

Hannah, Caleb, and Deacon nodded. Anya appreciated that although Caleb was hierarchically her superior, he was willing to let her lead. This kind of thing was her strength.

Hannah advised, "I can trigger them from a distance."

Anya considered it and decided it was a good plan. "Have at it."

Hannah unlimbered her shotgun. "Voltaic, can you feed me an overlay of their location?" A moment later, she pulled the trigger, and a heavy slug flew out of the shotgun, slammed into the right-side wall, and caused a massive explosion. Rock shot out and rained down as fire splashed against the force shields.

Anya commented, "Nice."

Hannah grinned. "I like making things explode." She took out five more the same way, another in the right wall, and two each in the ceiling and left wall.

Anya was surprised that none were set in the floor and focused her efforts on watching for things there. She marked the pressure plate she found in the virtual displays so everyone could step over it, and located a trip wire beyond it, right where one would naturally step when avoiding the plate. She growled, "Clever bastards, whoever did this. Someone definitely doesn't want us going this way. I hope we get to meet them soon so I can show them how much I appreciate their thoroughness."

Caleb observed, "This doesn't feel like the place a corporation would have."

Anya replied, "Maybe they hired out."

Voltaic interjected, "I'll look into that once you're all safe."

They continued evading traps until they reached a corridor that ran perpendicular to the one they were in. Caleb and Anya used fiber-optic cameras to check around the corners. Seeing nothing, they nonetheless reinforced their shields before stepping into the hallway. An instant later, magic slammed into them from both sides.

Anya snapped, "Contact."

Onyx trailed Jilly, Danica, and Billie as they moved down the corridor, thinking she needed some armor now that she'd seen the dragon's invulnerability. At an intersection, Danica and Billie checked the path ahead with cameras.

Danica reported, "I don't see anything, but I have a bad feeling about this."

Billie asked, "How about some dust?"

Onyx replied, "What kind?"

"Do you have anything that will get through shields?"

"Probably not."

"Something simple, then. We'll keep the cool stuff for later. Toss it in the middle of the intersection."

As Onyx crushed the studs, she noted Billie tapping her chest and pointing to the right, then gesturing toward Danica and pointing to the left. The leader of the Spellbound team nodded.

Onyx tossed the dust into the corridor, and they blew it in each direction. She stuck her head out and checked both ways, seeing ripples in each direction. "Magicals."

Jilly flashed by her, curving toward the left. Danica followed the dragon, and Billie followed Onyx as she dashed to the right, pulling her weapons as she headed for where she had spotted the shimmer. When she judged she was close, she leapt, raised both clubs over her head, and brought them down where she thought she'd seen the magical.

She hit a force shield but had prepared for it and still brought her clubs down hard as she got knocked backward. Billie was thinking along the same wavelength and stabbed Dorian at the ripple. The magical's invisibility dropped, probably a result of them being distracted by the foot of steel sticking into their chest.

Onyx landed on her back, vaulted to her feet, dashed

forward, and delivered a flying kick to the magical that knocked them off the blade. She landed a foot away from where her foe hit the wall, reached for her belt, grabbed a stud, and sprinkled tranquilizer dust over him. "Nice blade work."

Billie replied, "Dorian says it was all him."

Onyx laughed. "Naturally."

Anya charged toward the right and fired the grapnel on her right forearm ahead of her. It struck something invisible and hit the floor, revealing her opponent's location. She slammed a wave of force into the wall that caused stone to fly out and batter against her foe's shield. That distracted them enough that they became visible, and she rained down punches and kicks, her force-covered limbs slamming into the tight shield her foe had wrapped around himself. His outer shield had failed under the assault of the rocks.

It took thirty seconds, but she prevented the other magical from casting and finally broke through his shield. Her fist crashed against his nose, and blood spurted out. His hands went up instinctively, opening the way for her boot to slam up into his crotch and send him to the floor. She blasted him with lightning to keep him down, then spun to see that Deacon was behind her. Caleb and Hannah had handled the enemy in the other tunnel.

A noise from her original direction caused Anya to spin again. "This way." She dashed into a room that appeared empty until she used force magic to throw dust, dirt, and debris all around. Two figures appeared nearby with a third farther away. She threw a wave of force magic at them, and it knocked the closer pair backward.

The rectangular room was deeper than it was wide and seemed to be filled with cast-off bits of metal. Those lifted and spun in a blizzard between the figure in the back and the two enemies in the front.

Hannah's shotgun barked, and a slug flew at the nearer of the front two, only to be intercepted by a piece of metal that knocked it off target. Instead of hitting the target squarely, it glanced off their shield at shoulder height. It was still enough to distract them, and a moment later, the explosive Hannah threw detonated at their feet and sent them stumbling backward. Force shields were good but could still be overloaded if you hit them hard enough.

Caleb fired anti-magic rounds at the other one. Although the metal pieces flew into place to protect him from the initial barrage, the figure dropped when Anya added her rifle to the mix. She shifted her aim to the one in the back, but the whirlwind of metal protected the figure, as did the large pile of metal he was mostly hidden behind.

She continued to fire, pausing only when she had to reload, as did her allies, but the metal continued to get in the way of any shot with a chance of connecting. She realized it felt like a stalemate at the same moment she realized that didn't make any sense. She shouted a warning and spun as new attackers engaged from behind.

Caleb spun too, and together they hosed down the hallway while Hannah and Deacon continued their efforts against the person in the back of the room. Caleb slumped against the wall when the shots were done, bleeding from his chest. She ran to assist, but he was already fumbling in his belt for a healing potion.

"I'll be fine. Go deal with the bad guy."

Anya turned back to the figure in the room, who had stepped out and revealed herself to be a witch in a dark cloak. Long, curly black hair escaped from her cowl to lie over her shoulders and chest. A wave of her wand sent all the metal flying at them. Anya wrapped herself in shields and threw force magic to deflect some of them as her allies did the same. When the barrage was over, the woman had disappeared. "Hell. Watch out, wicked witch on the loose."

CHAPTER NINETEEN

Billie acknowledged the wicked witch comment as she waited for Danica and Jilly to return. They had reported that their enemy was down and were checking the tunnel. Her map filled in with a dead end as the two ran back.

Danica announced, "It looks like we have an opening ahead, according to the map."

Voltaic replied, "Confirmed, and everything else seems to be closed off."

Billie instructed, "Shadow, your team should return to the center to reinforce them. If everything's good, one or two of you can come join us."

Anya replied, "Affirmative."

Billie and Danica walked beside each other as they headed down the hallway, moving slowly to allow their scanners to search for traps ahead. The enemy knew they were here, so maintaining secrecy was no longer a concern and they could afford to move more slowly.

Danica muttered, "Should have brought a tank."

Billie replied, "Would have been hard to get down the shaft."

"More drones then. All the drones."

Onyx asked, "Where's the fun in that?"

Jilly echoed, "Yeah, where's the fun in that?"

Danica wiped sweat from her brow with the back of a glove. "We're all crazy to do this work."

Billie nodded. "Yep. But it's good crazy."

Danica chuckled. "Is it? Is it really?"

Their conversation quieted as the passage broadened ahead. They approached the large room cautiously and saw five figures inside. The four in the front looked virtually identical, clad in robes of dark orange and yellow with their faces shrouded and wands in their hands. A larger figure wearing a far more ornate robe in gorgeous crimson and deep black stood behind them.

Billie called, "Surrender now, and no harm will come to you."

All five figures laughed, and the four in front stepped back into combat postures.

Billie growled, "Why does that never work?"

Jilly replied, "Because they're stupid." She flashed past on the way into the room.

"You all take care of the trash. I'll deal with the big guy." Billie took two steps forward and launched herself into the air, taking advantage of the room's domed ceiling to evade the front defenders.

Jilly flew at the one on the end of the front four. He waved his wand at her and created a scorching beam of fire she easily avoided. She flew a loop around it to show her contempt for the attack. As she neared, he covered everything but his eyes in a flaming shield and summoned a wall of flame in front of her. Jilly curled up so the only thing exposed was her scales and plunged through the barrier.

She had aimed at the man's chest, but when she didn't hit him, she realized he had moved. She uncurled, climbed suddenly to avoid the next lance of fire that sought her, and dove at his face.

He flinched as she'd expected, and she whipped over his shoulder, then curved back. One of her favorite targets on any foe was the back of the leg, and she slashed her talons across the back of his knee. He buckled, screaming. He raised an arm to defend himself as she attacked again, and she landed on it, digging her claws deep into his forearm.

He released his wand as his muscles spasmed, and she bit his hand for good measure. Then she hopped off, grabbed the wand, flew with it to the mouth of the room, and tossed it down the hallway before returning to the fight.

Billie landed in front of the big guy and lifted her rifle. She shot six bullets at his chest, but they each flicked up before reaching him. He laughed as he pulled his cowl back, and she saw that he was bigger than she'd realized. A helmet in the same crimson and black motif as his robe covered his entire face. Billie drew Dorian with one hand and lobbed a grenade at him with the other, but it met the same fate as her bullets had, flying up and detonating harmlessly above.

He was motionless as she charged in and delivered her best kick with a force-covered shin to the outer part of his leg, which, if she connected properly, would numb it out. Again, he laughed at her attack.

Billie backpedaled uncertainly. "Uh-oh. Big guy's gonna be a problem."

Onyx had been momentarily distracted by the screaming resulting from Jilly's attack on the enemy next to hers but now had her head back in the game. She reached for her belt and picked a dust she'd never used before, something designed to be sticky and for use against small foes that could be trapped in it. She realized that while her enemy was shrouded in shields, they had to get air somehow. Maybe the dust would mess with that. The handful she threw doubled and redoubled in size as it flew toward her target.

The dust coated them, extinguishing the flame shield and leaving them cocooned. She pulled her clubs and moved toward the next, but was forced to spin away as a wash of flame exploded from the one she'd coated, blasting away her dust and threatening to burn her. The frantic dodge cost her her balance, and she spun down to the ground, but still got to her knees and dove out of the way as her other opponent blasted flame into where she'd been.

As she whipped her club around at the closer of the two, she snarled, "What is it with you guys and fire?" The blow lacked strength, but it connected with his kneecap and dropped him howling to the floor. She threw herself forward, still on her hands and knees, and brought both clubs down on his chest. Ribs broke, and she pressed one of the clubs into his stomach for leverage to get back to her feet. "Jerk." Then she turned toward the other one. "All right, you, let's dance."

———

Billie's foe whipped his robe off and threw it at her head. She released a burst of flame through Dorian that consumed it before it reached her and found her opponent standing before her in a full suit of armor with two flaming scimitars in his hands. She recalculated his size again. There must have been no space under that robe, and it must have been straining to hold him in.

He strode forward arrogantly and slashed a scimitar down at her. She stepped to the side and blocked with Dorian, shifting the blow beyond where it would have hit her. The other one came in at her head, and she flicked her fingers to summon a burst of force to knock it over her head. She backpedaled, using force magic to redirect each of his blows, sure that trying to meet his powerful strikes with direct blocks would be a bad idea.

She stabbed with Dorian several times, but the only time a blow got through his defenses, it scraped off his armor and failed to mar the sheen of the overlapping scales. She realized he'd driven her back toward one of the initial four hooded figures only when she caught a new attack out of the corner of her eye. She spun to block the new enemy and delivered a blast of force magic to his face that knocked him toward Onyx, who took a break from her opponent to smack him in the head with her club.

Fire blossomed along Billie's back as one of the scimitars sliced through her armor and into her skin. The flame was extra agony, and she screamed with the pain of it. Then Onyx was at her side, clubs knocking the giant man's next attack away.

Billie stumbled to the side and fumbled for her healing potion. Her legs collapsed as she freed it from the belt and brought it to her lips. As it did its work, she watched Jilly join the fight in time to keep Onyx from being overwhelmed.

The tiny dragon darted in and out, forcing the big man to use one of his scimitars to deter her. He suddenly backpedaled, and a wall of flame appeared in front of him. Billie threw ice on it, as did the other magicals, but when the steam vanished, he was gone. Billie snarled, "Damn it, who the hell was that guy?"

Voltaic sounded alarmed as she warned, "Massive heat buildup all around you."

Danica snapped, "Everyone portal out, now."

The portal to their staging point a block away had just closed behind them when the building went up in a pillar of fire that lit the nighttime sky as if it were day.

CHAPTER TWENTY

The next day, the teams got together for happy hour at a Cleveland bar Danica liked. They gathered in a back room, and one of the members of Danica's team explained that the place had supposedly been the site of a shootout involving Elliott Ness back in the day. The story was the high point of the session. Everyone was down since no one considered the day before to have been a success. Izzy and Voltaic talked in a corner, and the rest of the teams had paired off in twos.

Billie stood next to Danica, each of them with a beer bottle in their hands, and observed, "Our teams get along well. That's something."

Danica replied, "It's good to see. Somehow, I think Arthur will find opportunities for us to work together quite a lot in the future."

Billie laughed. "Shifting that cost burden over to the federal government, like Helen said."

"Yep. He's a master of that kind of thing."

"Well, I'd say Fire Guy and his minions are a legitimate

magical threat, so we're on the case until they're taken down. What do you plan to do?"

Danica shrugged. "One of the most annoying things about this gig is that we're mostly reactive. Mainly, we wind up waiting for the next attack while trying to get something that will give us a clue about what it might be. Voltaic will be on it, and I'll send my investigators in to talk to our client's company again, see if they have any more data on the other one."

"You didn't get anything from the place's servers?"

"No. Most of their stuff was too heavily encrypted to crack. Voltaic's systems are still going at it, but they haven't chewed through yet and might never. Finding that location was a lucky strike." She frowned. "Or maybe not. Maybe they left it there to draw in anyone who was looking. Leave us spinning our wheels while thinking we have something real."

"That's a dark thought, but you might be right." Billie shook her head. "We just need that first clue, the one that leads to all the others."

Danica looked thoughtful for a second. "Maybe I can help us get a clue. Are you available after dark?"

Billie laughed. "Are you asking me out on a date?"

Danica gave the joke the half-smile it deserved. "I thought you might like to meet a friend of mine. She's something."

"More something than Jilly?"

"No one's *that* something."

Billie laughed. "Sure. Can I bring Onyx?"

Danica raised an eyebrow. "Could you stop her from coming?"

Billie coughed on her drink. "Probably not."

The other woman laughed. "Then yes, you can."

When the gathering died down, they headed for Danica's house and shared one more drink in the backyard. When dusk arrived, Danica led her into the woods behind the house. They walked down the path until they encountered a shimmering portal.

Billie asked, "Did the portal come with the house?"

Danica chuckled. "I couldn't tell you. I felt drawn back here, and there it was. And apparently, she's willing to see you."

Billie's head tilted to the side as she asked intelligently, "Huh?"

"The portal isn't always in the same place, and it isn't always open."

Jilly added, "The other side of the portal is where Danica and I met." She landed on Danica's shoulder. "Let's go."

Time changed as they stepped through the portal, from dusk to late afternoon. The path continued on the far side, but tree branches with odd-shaped leaves crowned it. Overall, it felt claustrophobic.

Billie muttered, "Those trees seem ominous."

Danica replied, "They're pretty tame today. They can be mean."

"These trees are old. Like, really, really old. Where are we?" Onyx sounded impressed.

Danica replied, "Not sure. My best guess is Oriceran, but who knows. I've never been able to figure it out."

Jilly added, "Me neither."

After walking for fifteen minutes, they reached an oval-shaped clearing in front of a house that looked as if it had been grown, created by interlocking branches and roots that seamlessly formed walls.

A rocking chair stood near the door, and a woman sat in it. Her long white hair gave a first impression of age, but her unlined pale skin and bright eyes belied it. Black makeup colored her eyes and lips. Her smile at Jilly and Danica was full of affection as she asked, "What can I do for you and your friends, my student?"

Jilly flew to land on the arm of the chair. "This is Onyx. Onyx, this is Rowena."

Rowena smiled. "Welcome, pixie."

Onyx replied, "Thank you. This is all so beautiful."

"I see you appreciate my trees. Wonderful."

Danica added, "And this is Billie."

Rowena nodded. "Welcome to you, as well."

"We seek some guidance."

The corner of Rowena's mouth twitched up. "The cards?"

"Yes."

The older woman frowned theatrically. "You know, you owe me some training time."

Danica sighed. "Yes, I know, I'm an eternal disappointment."

Rowena laughed as she stood. "Let's go, then." A path behind the house took them through more canopies of menacing branches and to a rock wall set in a tall hill. Rowena tapped the wall with her wand, and a door etched with unfamiliar symbols appeared. She spoke words that slipped from Billie's mind an instant after hearing them and dabbed the carvings with blood.

The door opened to reveal a comfortable den. Candles flared to life, sending flickering illumination throughout the room. Soft music began to play. The wooden table in the center seemed to be the cross-section of a tree, polished to a soft glow.

Rowena gestured them toward the chairs.

Billie asked, "Are there usually four chairs? Because there doesn't seem to be room for them."

Danica shook her head. "No. The most I've seen is three."

"So, she knew we were coming?"

Danica sat in the farthest chair. "I have no idea what she knows, or how she knows it."

Rowena returned with a deck of cards wrapped in fabric. She unfolded the cloth and tapped her wand against the cards, then waved it at them. A breeze moved through the room, sending chills up Billie's back.

Onyx murmured, "Cool."

Rowena laughed. "I am. Quite." Another wave of the wand caused the cards to float in the air. The witch instructed, "Clear your minds, then focus on your questions."

Billie complied.

Six cards floated down to the table, then the rest of the deck reassembled itself in a stack on the fabric.

Rowena turned the cards over one by one, and when the array was complete, little explanation was needed. Each card had a villainous-looking figure holding a weapon on it. Three were set on watery landscapes, and the remainder showed fire in the background.

Danica noted, "Our enemies are connected, then."

Rowena replied, "The cards suggest it is so. Different elements, though. Fire and water."

Onyx observed, "Drugs and flame. Seems to align with what we've experienced lately."

Rowena restored her deck to its holding place, and they walked back to the clearing. They said their goodbyes and headed back down the path.

Billie remarked, "At least we have a confirmation of something. Let's stay in close touch."

Danica grinned and raised an eyebrow. "Are you asking me on a date, now?"

Billie laughed. "No, but apparently I'm really good at walking into traps, verbal included."

Onyx teased, "Okay, then you go first from now on."

Billie shook her head. "Fantastic."

CHAPTER TWENTY-ONE

The next morning, Billie and Caleb wandered down the hallway together with coffees in hand to meet with Eileen in her lab. The team's tech was visibly energetic, and Billie was jealous. Starting quickly in the morning was never a thing she'd been good at. Unless there was a monster to defeat, which got the adrenaline pumping in a way that caffeine could never match.

Eileen had added a new element to the room since Billie's last visit, a mannequin that held what looked like a slightly different version of her team's armor. She was about to ask about it, but Caleb greeted boisterously, "What have you got for us, brainiac?"

Eileen raised an eyebrow. "I'm sensing something. Yes, the IQ level in the room just dropped dramatically."

Caleb laughed. "I'm missing good slacking time at my desk for this. Make with the stuff."

Billie sipped her coffee. "I'm ready to be excited."

Eileen walked to the mannequin and lifted its arm. On the outside of the forearm, a tube ran along it from about wrist to elbow. It looked like it was plastic, but Billie was sure it would be of some more sophisticated material.

She asked, "What is it?"

Eileen replied, "Collapsible shield."

Billie frowned. "That small? I mean, it's big. On the suit. Kind of bulky, I mean."

Caleb advised, "Perhaps have some more coffee before you try to speak, boss."

She waved dismissively but took a long drink, knowing he was right.

Eileen laughed, brought over a leather vambrace that sported the same tube, and strapped it around Billie's arm. She stepped back. "Press the button. The activation will be verbal in the field, of course."

Billie set her coffee on a nearby shelf and pressed the button with her right hand. The shield unfurled like a sail, then snapped to rigidity. It covered her from the floor to above her head, and was the width of her body, more or less. "Holy hell."

Caleb walked around her to examine it. "Very cool. How does that work?"

Eileen replied, "It's memory fabric. Little chips tell it where to go. It knows two states, folded and unfolded, and in the latter case it locks into place and a current holds it there. Its usefulness is limited by how much power we can feed it. I'm working on improving that, but for now, it drains power quickly. About ninety seconds of use, assuming two deployments. It takes a little more power to activate and deactivate it than it does to maintain it."

Caleb scratched his chin with the hand that wasn't holding his coffee. "It eliminates the ability to attack or cast with the off hand, since you have to kind of curl the arm back around to position it in front of you."

Eileen countered, "It stops bullets, and you still have one hand free."

Billie pointed out, "We're likely using that hand already for other bullet deflectors, anyway."

Caleb shrugged. "Fair point."

"It is a little heavy. Going to make punching with this arm slow."

Eileen countered, "Yeah, but magicals have the ability to do whatever you do to get stronger. I call it juicing. That's probably not what you call it."

Billie laughed. "No, that's kind of a pejorative term, from, like, centuries ago."

Caleb noted, "I call it buffing."

Billie replied, "Pumping."

Eileen rolled her eyes. "Yeah, those are both much better. I thought you might be dubious, so I asked Quentin to lend a hand."

The scuff of a boot behind her caused Billie to turn toward the door in time to see the team's sniper walk in followed by their demolitions expert.

Quentin added, "And I asked Hannah to help out."

Billie scowled. "Were you waiting right outside the door? Eavesdropping? Like some sort of criminals?"

Quentin shook his head. "No, down the hall." He tapped his ear. "But open comm, so we've been listening in."

Billie put her hands on her hips. "I've been set up. Rude."

Quentin laughed. "Well, I think you'll appreciate the result." He opened the box he carried and handed over a modified version of the team's standard pistol. A blocky rectangle that was a little wider than the rest of the gun was positioned under and slightly in front of the barrel.

Billie handed it to Caleb, who looked it over. "I'll bite. What is it?"

"Micro-grenade launcher."

Hannah held out her hand, palm up, to display the ammunition for it, which looked like miniature darts with silver tips and different-colored bodies. "We've tested several different kinds of rounds, and it looks like fire, flash-bang, and smoke have the most utility. You push the selector lever and pull the same trigger."

Quentin added, "The packs are modular and work with the pistol's rail system. Slide this one off, slide a new one on, and you're ready to go again."

Caleb remarked, "This is seriously cool. Y'all are clever."

Billie teased, "Everyone seems clever to you, Caleb, because of the IQ thing."

He grunted dramatically. "Me smart."

Eileen observed, "It seems like the new pistol balances out some of the lost offensive capability from the shield, and obviously the shield is a more reliable way for magicals and nonmagicals both to handle enemies with anti-magic ammunition. You can close with the shield in front of you and fire your pistol or throw actual grenades around it, then collapse the shield to fight if you need to."

Hannah replied, "I've been meaning to ask. What happens if the shield doesn't close properly?"

Eileen nodded. "Smart question. There's an eject function that will respond to the proper voice command."

Billie swung her arm experimentally and threw a

couple of punches. "You're right. With a little magical support, it'll be like it wasn't there at all. I'm sold."

Eileen grinned. "Good, because I already modified the holsters on the equipment belts for the pistols and added additional power to the suit."

Billie looked at Caleb. "Am I even in charge here?"

He grinned. "Nope, you're a figurehead. I'm the real power."

"Excellent, real power. Figure out where the hell that fire dude came from, stat."

He raised his hands. "Me not that smart. You power."

She chuckled. "I thought so." She unclipped the vambrace and handed it back.

Eileen added, "Also, Anya mentioned the bird drone the Spellbound team used. I don't know why Izzy and I didn't think of that. It's such a good idea. I'm printing up a new model of our mini drone based on Spellbound's designs. It should be ready to go next week."

Billie nodded. "And the rest of the stuff?"

"Is ready to go now."

Billie clapped, then reclaimed her coffee and toasted with it. "Awesome, because I think we're going to need every advantage we can get."

CHAPTER TWENTY-TWO

Saturday morning, Billie and Onyx walked into Ethan's shop twenty minutes before their appointed meeting time with Kalani. Billie was second-guessing her decision to accept the other woman's offer to teach her, as she had a dozen times already that day. Onyx was just excited and proudly showed off her new bow and the quiver full of arrows on her back.

Ethan asked, "What are you hunting?"

"Evil fire guys, hopefully."

He chuckled. "If you'd warned me ahead of time, I could have tried to make a potion that protects you from flame."

Billie asked, "Really?"

He shook his head. "Probably not. It's amazing how much time researching a new potion takes, and most alchemists are unwilling to share their recipes, for obvious reasons."

Billie handed over a sheet of paper with a web address on it. "If you go here, you'll be able to find a new recipe. It's something a witch we're working with came up with. She says it's a proactive healing potion, meaning you can take it before a fight, and it lasts in the system twenty minutes or so."

He whistled. "Are you serious?"

Billie nodded. "Completely. But there's one caveat. You can only make it for me and my team for now. When and if Lilac gets the patent up and running, she's willing to talk to you about being her DC connection."

"That's icing on the cake. I would do it just for the learning."

Onyx laughed. "That's exactly how Lilac said you'd respond."

Elaine urged, "Off with you. Get to the back room and do your work. I'll help them." As he bustled away, she shook her head. "He gets excited, and it's like all logic and functional thought leaves his head. So, I have your resupply of healing potions ready. Do you need energy?"

Billie shook her head. "We're still fully stocked. Also, while I'll still come around to visit, I'm going to shift the logistical responsibility for our potions over to my new admin, Justin. You'll like him."

Elaine smiled. "As long as the money's good, I don't care who does the paying."

"He'll set up a way for us to transfer the money to you, too. But for now, here's a check."

She handed it over, and the other woman nodded. "Perfect. I'll get them." She headed for the back room at the same moment the bell on the front door rang.

Billie and Onyx both turned to see Kalani enter. The elf was dressed more informally than usual in a matching zippered top and bottoms that looked like the softest black fabric ever created. Her long black hair was in a braid that hung over her shoulder, and her pointed ears held a total of ten silver stud earrings.

Billie thought the way the other woman looked at her was like a cat sizing up a mouse it was about to kill, but her smile seemed genuine as she asked, "Ready?"

Billie replied, "As ready as I'm going to be."

Onyx added, "I'm way more ready than her."

Kalani laughed. "Excellent." She opened a portal that showed an expansive lawn on the opposite side. When they walked through, she turned, and they did the same. Before them was a building that wasn't quite a mansion but was way larger than any normal house had any right to be. Perfectly manicured lawns spread out on all sides except for where a curving driveway led up to the four-car garage.

Billie whistled, and Onyx commented, "Whatever you do, it must pay really well."

Kalani laughed. "Family money that I'm lucky to have. Of course, I have to live with my family to enjoy it, so there's a balance there. But it gives me a lot of good space to work in."

As Kalani led them around the side of the house toward the backyard, Billie asked, "So what are you going to teach me?"

Kalani chuckled and shook her head. "Always leaving the door wide open for a counter. I hope you fight better than you talk."

Billie winced at the realization that she'd left herself open again for a verbal riposte. "I hope so, too."

"We'll find out shortly."

Billie was amazed by how large the backyard was

when they reached it. Trees surrounded the grassy expanse on the right and at the back, but the left was bounded by a giant hedge, easily twelve feet high. It ran irregularly, going straight for most of the distance before kicking away from what she presumed was the property line.

The arrangement made little sense until Kalani led them to it, waved, and muttered a command word. The hedges moved apart, as did another row behind them that she hadn't known was there, giving them a path through.

On the opposite side was a training space that looked well-used. A large sandy area with a perimeter defined by flowers was on the left side as they walked in, and Billie recognized that it was the same size as martial arts tournament mats. To the right, humanoid targets stood sixty feet away, seventy-five feet away, and one hundred feet away, to judge by the numbers above their heads. Apart from that, the area was all well-tended grass. It gave the sense of being disconnected from the outside world, and Billie said so.

Kalani replied, "A little extra magic helps, dampening the sound while still letting all the air and breeze through. But yes, this is my place. No one gets in without my permission."

Onyx asked, "What if they came in over the top?"

Kalani's grin was predatory. "Ward spells would activate, and they'd wish they hadn't."

Onyx nodded. "Noted. Okay. Don't wander off at Kalani's house, check."

The elf laughed as she gestured toward the fighting area. "Take your boots off, and we'll spar a little. The sand feels way better on bare feet, and it's grippier that way, too."

Kalani rolled up her khaki military pants several times so her legs were visible from just below the knee down. Billie did the same, grateful that she'd worn loose-fitting clothes in anticipation of something like this.

Kalani dropped back into a defensive stance that Billie thought was most similar to karate. "Put up force shields for protection, and you may begin."

Billie slid forward and tested the waters with a moderate roundhouse kick from her lead leg at Kalani's midsection. The other woman circled away and threw an equally slow front kick at Billie. She blocked down with a circular motion, then jumped in and tried an elbow to the other woman's head.

Kalani had turned with the motion of the block and spun away from the attack. Billie judged her movement style as indirect, but then the woman skipped in and delivered a solid side kick right to Billie's ribs, sneaking it in before her elbow came down to block. Billie staggered backward, then countered, and they exchanged several more blows.

Then Kalani raised a hand. "Stop."

Billie stepped away, as one always did during formal combat matches. Kalani observed, "You're fast. Not as fast as me, but that's fine. You need to be more precise, though. Think in straight lines. That side kick was a direct, shortest distance attack. That's the type of thing you need to embrace."

Billie scratched her cheek with a knuckle. "You lulled

me in with the slow pace, and I lost my focus on technique."

"Good, and that trick won't fool you ever again, I'm sure. Now, let's add some offensive magic to the mix."

They fought again, this time with Kalani kicking off the attack. The other woman came in behind a blast of force that sprayed sand up at Billie and blocked her view. She backpedaled quickly, getting out of the way before the other woman's kick came through the cloud.

As Kalani set her foot down, Billie flicked her fingers to try to knock the other woman off-balance. Her offensive magic struck her opponent's defensive magic and failed to penetrate. She grinned and threw herself into the fight. They traded kicks and punches, both with actual fists and with fists of force disconnected from their bodies.

Billie was the first to go down when Kalani used a force sweep to cut her legs out from underneath her, but she immediately flipped back up and used three force bolts in a row to pummel the other woman in three spots. Kalani's shields held up against the first two, but the third knocked her off-balance. Billie tried to take advantage of it, but Kalani was immediately back on her feet.

She called a stop and grinned. "Good raw material. We can do better, though. Take a rest."

Billie realized she was breathing hard. *Too much desk work, not enough running.* A daily run had been a routine part of every day in the AET. Maybe she would need to institute that for her new team as well. She laughed at the idea of how Izzy would respond to that decision.

Billie watched as Onyx held out her bow to Kalani, who

took it, drew it, and nodded appreciatively. "Excellent craftsmanship."

Onyx replied, "It's warded for accuracy and strength. I only brought standard arrows today. I have some cool special ones, too."

Kalani crossed her arms. "All right, let me see you shoot."

Billie was impressed at the smoothness with which Onyx drew an arrow from her quiver, nocked it to the string, drew, and released. It wasn't the fastest archery she'd ever seen, but for someone she presumed was out of practice or had no previous training in archery, it was great.

The first arrow smacked into the sign that said seventy-five feet.

Kalani chuckled. "Focus on accuracy, not speed. Speed will come."

The next arrow went into the head of the closest one, then Onyx followed up with similar shots at the more distant targets, neither of which hit the bullseye, marked where the nose would be. Kalani stepped forward. "Nock an arrow and draw it back."

Onyx complied, and Kalani reached out and gently adjusted her arm positioning. "Your bow has the power, and you have the strength. You don't need to do a high arc to hit at this distance. Think in straight lines and trust yourself."

Onyx took a deep breath, then released the arrow. It thudded into the center of the bullseye on the medium distance target. The pixie broke into a smile. "Thank you."

Kalani nodded. "Of course. Here's another thing. Pixies

are magical by nature, so your power responds to your will. Use that. Picture the arrow hitting where it needs to hit, then imagine the path it has to take. Your magic will respond and help your body conform to a shot that travels the path."

"That's what the elders said."

Kalani clapped Onyx on the shoulder. "Then they've shown the wisdom of age. Always nice when that works out." She turned to Billie. "Okay, now let's take a look at your dagger."

Billie picked up Dorian from where she'd set him before her bout with Kalani, drew the blade from its sheath, and sat cross-legged in the grass across from the other woman. She set the blade between them, and both laid their fingers on it.

A moment later, Dorian appeared between them as if he was really in the world with them. He appeared as he had the first time they'd met, dressed all in black with a gorgeous black on black embroidered coat that reached his ankles. His shining black hair reached to his waist. He bared his white teeth in an arrogant smile at Kalani, then asked Billie, "Why am I here?"

Kalani replied, "I'm trying to help Billie better understand the shape-change magic that you possess. Can you show me?"

Dorian's grin became almost malicious. He flicked his hand, and Kalani's head rocked back. Billie didn't know how she avoided falling over.

The moment hung, then the other woman slowly brought her head forward, eyes burning into Dorian's with a glare that would have sent Billie running. "Impertinent."

"You're not my wielder."

"I'm an ally."

"That's yet to be proven."

In a deceptively soft tone, Kalani observed, "I could melt you down and turn you into earrings."

Dorian matched her tone. "I don't believe my wielder would allow that."

Instead of replying, Kalani removed her hands. Billie did the same, and Dorian's avatar vanished.

Kalani divulged, "He showed me how it works, despite being a jerk. It's like any other kind of channeled magic. The more you do it, the more the channel will establish and solidify, and the less effort it will take to travel it. Like a stream, carving out a path through rock. Put a little effort into it every day, and soon you'll be able to do it at will."

Billie asked, "Really?"

"I have no reason to lie to you." Then Kalani's voice changed. "Or do I?" She laughed. "I've called for refreshments to be brought out back. Let's go have some cold tea and discuss what else you might like to learn."

CHAPTER TWENTY-THREE

Deacon leaned back in the expensive autonomous car he'd rented for this visit. He was pretending to be a journalist who wrote for high-end publications, so he needed to travel in a style appropriate to the role. He needed to dress that way as well and was clad in a sharp black suit paired with a black shirt and a red tie. Beside him, Prem Patel wore khakis and a sports coat appropriate to his role as photographer. Inside his bag were the infomancy relays that were the reason for today's visit.

Deacon asked, "Z, are you sure you got the meeting on the calendar?"

Izzy replied, "You need to stop whining and quit worrying. It's there. Settle down."

"Yeah, you're not the one who's in trouble if the system flags us."

"It's not going to flag you."

"So you've been inside their security system and can guarantee it?"

Annoyance colored her voice. "Don't be a jerk."

Deacon laughed as the car stopped. He got out, waited for Prem to bustle around from the opposite side of the vehicle, and strolled forward. Izzy had warned him this company was likely to have sophisticated scanners that might detect comms, so she would trickle data to their lenses if she needed to communicate with them but not interact verbally. He was fine with that. Avoiding detection was a good thing.

He held the lobby door open for Prem, who responded with a small nod as he bustled through, indicating that he'd placed the first of the infomancy relays outside the building as planned. Deacon felt the oppressive press of an anti-magic field as they entered the lobby. He wasn't using magic, so it wasn't an operational issue, but the feeling was still uncomfortable.

The lobby was a grand affair, three stories high with a massive steampunk-style chandelier lighting fixture standing in for the sun. Everything was chrome, glass, and steel except for the marble tile underfoot.

The sensor arch that covered the doorways was a work of art, like an undulating ocean wave they walked beneath. No alarms went off that he could detect, but before they were allowed to proceed, the guards waved them over to inspect the photography equipment.

He was sure they had already X-rayed both of them as they walked through the arch, but backup checks were a logical precaution. Pharmaceutical companies were logically extra concerned about security, given the types of research they conducted.

The guards took each item out of the bag, then felt the lining. They opened the two cases full of tiny cards, half of which looked like memory chips, and the other half like small batteries. They removed those items from the camera, put in replacements, and turned it on to ensure it worked. When it did, they repacked the bag exactly as it had been and returned it to Prem.

Deacon saw the relief on the other man's face because he was looking for it. The cards and power supplies worked as they were supposed to because Izzy and Eileen had predicted the guards would check. But they were also the relays that needed to be placed around so Izzy could hack the company's server.

The goal was to figure out how the company was related to the fire magical they faced and to support Spellbound's efforts in the same direction. The why of it wasn't really his concern, but accomplishing it was.

A guard escorted them to the desk, where a beaming brunette with overly red lips, a tight business suit that looked entirely natural on her, and notably high heels greeted them.

"I'm Christine. Pleased to meet you. We have IDs for you. Please loop them around your necks. Also, please leave your phones at the desk."

They complied, and she continued. "I was surprised to see this meeting on my calendar today. Seems like it was added at the very last minute. Normally I would have been more prepared. What are we meeting about?"

Deacon put on his most polished smile. This was the element he was best in, ingratiating himself with people, sliding his way in and out of places he shouldn't be, and generally lying his face off. He loved it, so this profession had been a natural choice. "I've been assigned as a freelancer to cover the current bleeding edge of medical technology. Obviously, drugs are going to be one of the primary angles of interest for the story."

Christine nodded. "We do more than drugs these days, but certainly you're in the right place. Do you have a medical background?"

He couldn't bluff being a doctor. "Only medical reporting. But I've learned a lot along the way. I'll let you know if you talk over my head. Also, is it okay if my colleague shoots pictures as we go along?"

"Certainly, in most areas. I'll alert you ahead of time if somewhere needs to remain confidential." She took them down a long hallway that was dotted with portraits of the CEOs who had been in charge of the company through the two hundred years of its existence. He nodded as if interested as she spoke about them. Part of his brain kept a loose eye on Prem as he took pictures and also planted infomancy devices.

The other man had hung back to do so again when Christine warned, "You both need to stay close. If your badge isn't in proximity to mine, security will have a fit, and angry men with guns will materialize out of the walls." She leaned over and added conspiratorially, "If you ask me, they're a little tightly wound."

Deacon replied, "Given what you do here, it seems like corporate espionage would be a constant risk. I guess they have their work cut out for them." At her nod, he added, "That's one of the angles of my article, actually. Do you have any particular experience with corporate espionage?"

She raised a perfectly manicured eyebrow. "Are you asking me if I'm a spy?" Then she laughed. "My only experience with it has been as part of the planning to keep confidential things confidential. We don't condone such activities as a company. And frankly, we don't need to. We're years ahead of our nearest competition."

Christine led them into a corridor filled with the various innovations the company had come up with over the years, and Deacon realized he was basically on a standard tour designed to impress visitors. It included a third hallway with some descriptions of the lives they'd saved and the charitable things they had done. That brought them back out to the lobby, and he feared that would be the end of the tour.

Christine walked to the elevator and pressed her ID against a pad. When they exited the car, she requested, "No pictures here, please," and Prem obligingly put the camera away.

They stood on a metal catwalk that ringed a large rectangular room. It had stairs at each of the cardinal directions. Below, glassed-in chambers filled the space, tied to a central corridor that would allow them to get from one to the other. Each also had its own airlock entrance and exit, as did the central corridor.

Deacon asked, "What kind of stuff requires this level of protection?" Then he grinned. "Are you hiding nuclear weapons here?"

Christine chuckled. "No, none of that. But everything we work with these days requires this level of protection. It's all genetic modification and viruses now, and we definitely wouldn't want that getting out."

He frowned and said directly, as a reporter would, "I

suppose that would make for a formidable weapon on the battlefield."

Christine nodded. "It could, in many ways. Of course, the Geneva Convention prevents direct use of such agents on enemy troops."

"Of course."

"Plus, they don't do much against robots."

He chuckled. It was true that more and more armies were mechanical. "Makes sense." His mind was locked on a previous thought. *You can't use it against enemy troops, but you could use it to create supersoldiers, like people have been trying to do forever. I wonder what that would look like. Maybe a big fire dude?*

She walked them around the catwalk and explained some of the things they were working on below. This floor was not the deep research section unless she was lying about the research. The elevator hadn't had any buttons or indicators, so he had no way of knowing how many levels were beneath this one. At a guess, he would say there were probably a lot of them.

After they had made it all the way around, Christine took them to her office, where he asked appropriate questions for his reporter persona and Prem took pictures. When they finally exited the building, both waited until they were in the car to discuss the visit, and even then only did so after Izzy advised through their comms, "You're clear of listening devices and your phones weren't messed with."

Billie joined the line and asked, "What did you get?"

He shared a brief summary of the tour. "Genetic manipulation seems like something that could be worth looking into."

Billie replied, "I agree. Izzy, get to that looking into thing."

The infomancer replied, "The chances of me getting in there and not being noticed are small. I mean, I know we set it up for a reason, but you should be aware."

"I'm sure you'll figure something out."

"I appreciate how your faith in me is always directly proportional to how much you need me to do a thing."

Billie laughed. "I always appreciate you, Z."

"Uh-huh. Prove it. Love me with money."

Deacon stifled a laugh and saw that Prem was doing the same. Billie replied, "You'll have to talk to Justin about that."

Izzy countered, "Exactly what I thought you'd say. I'm going to embezzle what I need from your bank account. That'll teach you."

"You know, warning of a crime before you do it isn't actually very smart."

"Or is it a mastermind-level move, so beyond your comprehension that you can't fathom it?"

"Stop giving me a headache by being a headache and get to work."

"Yeah, yeah. Right on, boss." Satisfaction filled Izzy's voice.

CHAPTER TWENTY-FOUR

Izzy sat behind her computers after a nap, a decent meal, and several energy drinks. She would have to be at the top of her game tonight if she was going to hack into Genovary's corporate servers. In her experience, even government agencies didn't deploy the kind of defensive measures that big corporations did. Add to that the intellectual property concerns of a company that was both a defense contractor and a pharmaceutical developer, mix in the fact that they were probably doing something unethical if not illegal, and she expected a serious challenge.

Every problem had to start with a first move. For her, that meant setting up a false trail, so if anyone detected her, there would be something to justify her presence there. She headed into the usual places where quality info-mancers found work. Not the more public low-level boards, but the hidden, private ones where those with real skills found those with the need for them.

She visited all she knew and seeded threads with a request for someone to make a run against the corporation. She never used it by name since that would be too obvious, but someone looking for a trail would find it, and hopefully believe it. She had broken the security on some of the sites years before, and in those servers, she falsely aged the posts. In the others, she changed the wording to make it appear as though the mysterious figure seeking infomancy assistance was becoming desperate. Some threads would lead to dead ends, and others to disreputable brokers who wouldn't be believed when they claimed to have nothing to do with the posting.

Her best threads, the ones she hoped would convince them, led back to a military weapons contractor that was new on the scene and was a plausible candidate for trying to compromise the corporation. After she had done all she could think of, she reviewed her actions and decided she'd muddied the field enough that nobody could easily trace her. That took care of legitimizing the run.

She submersed herself fully into her computers, and Nakano's arming room materialized around her as she left the real world and entered the simulated one. She had considered deploying as Alloy but decided that maintaining her professional and personal separation was essential, even for a rush she was trying to have deniability for. The space felt like home and was her own design, drawing upon several real-world and fictional Japanese temples.

She stood in the exact center of the place on a dark wood floor a few steps below the rest of the room. Shoji panels filled the outer perimeter, lit as if sunlight was beyond them. Vases held bonsai trees to add to the atmosphere. The most important things in the room were the three armor stands and the one statue with its arms outstretched, each located at a corner of this lower level.

She moved first to the stand that held her body armor. Her avatar had materialized in the black fabric base layer, and each piece of her armor went on over it. Strapping them on was like a ritual.

As she put each piece in place, the smaller pieces rippled as the tiny robotic elements self-tested to ensure they were ready. Visually, it looked like ancient samurai armor, but she moved much more freely than those who wore the real stuff did, and it was far more protective. She drew on the heavy boots and buckled them into place.

Properly attired and filled with confidence from it, she headed to the next armor stand. She slipped on the long black skirt that hung almost to her ankles, then added the gray tunic with its embroidered dragon in bold colors. She tied a black cloth belt into an elaborate knot to hold the tunic closed over her armor.

The next statue extended her katana in its hands, and she took it, holding it up to examine the blade. It shone in the false sunlight from the shoji panels as she moved it through the air, then slid perfectly into the scabbard on her back.

From the last armor stand, she took two silver discs imprinted with the same dragon as on her chest. She set one on each shoulder, where they remained when she removed her hand. A mental command caused a cloak that reached her feet to flow out of them. A cowl hanging at her back would allow her to hide her face.

She headed for one of the shoji panels and slid it aside. Beyond was her avatar's technology space. It resembled the outer room but held things that one did not. Unusually, she selected one of the guns and slid it into the holster at the small of her back, under the tunic and cloak. She generally didn't carry one since they didn't fit the motif, but she wasn't sure what she would come up against, and firepower was always handy.

A stack of shelves held grenades, tiny enough that three would fit in her palm simultaneously. They clipped onto holders in the belt portion of her armor, where they looked like ornaments. She opened the inner forearm of her left gauntlet and slid a lockpick set inside, then added a small medkit to the one on the right.

Finally, she slipped a throwing knife into the outer forearm of each gauntlet. She clapped her hands three times, and the simulation fell away, leaving her hovering over the nighttime cityscape of the magical dark web. If she knew where the server was, this was when she would fly to it and begin her assault. However, since she didn't have that information, she headed instead to a place where she might discover it.

One of the best places she knew to find information about American defense contractors was hidden in a part of the magical dark web that resembled Germany at the end of the Cold War. She wasn't sure why someone had made that decision, but it had caught on, and there were several such bars.

She landed outside a bar named Zeitgeist in purple cursive script. The neon buzzed intermittently above the entrance. Its façade was a mix of old and new, appropriate to the time. Original weathered blocks sat next to new concrete ones, and other materials repurposed from fallen buildings, she presumed. The few windows on its face were blocked by curtains, preventing any glimpse of what lay inside.

A small alley ran beside the bar, and as she walked past it toward the door, she noticed graffiti adorned much of the walls near the opening. Some of it was modern while other parts seemed to refer to World War II.

As always, the quality of the atmosphere impressed her. Inside, the walls were original brick and the wood floor creaked underfoot, but everything was clean and warm, something she wouldn't have anticipated from the exterior. The track lighting above provided overall illumination but also drew the eyes to various portraits and propaganda posters on the wall. The bar stood out as an anachronism, gleaming chrome and glass that would have been more appropriate in a nightclub.

Bottles behind the bar were in languages that Nakano didn't know, but her software translated them. The stools lining the bar were modern chrome with black leather seats, but the person she was looking for wasn't among the few people sitting there.

Near the rear of the place, a small, elevated section held several booths, oriented in a way to provide a sight line to the entrance, and her quarry was seated in one of them. Her footsteps beat in time with a 1970s David Bowie song. As she arrived, the music transitioned into an industrial piece by Kraftwerk, an amusing bias on the part of whoever had coded this place.

Nakano took a seat across the table from the blonde woman whose short hair did nothing to damage her femininity. The cigarette the other woman placed between her red-painted lips and drew upon glowed almost as brightly as her eyes. She had encountered the woman in the past and knew her to have a particular interest in undermining the United States. She would have the server address of a military contractor if anyone would. She didn't need to know that Nakano's purpose was different than the undermining she might hope for. "Incache."

The other woman nodded. "Nakano. Been a while."

"I'm looking for some information."

"Of course you are. That's the only time you visit."

She lifted an eyebrow. "Are you saying you'd like to pursue a relationship that's more than transactional?"

The other woman laughed and stubbed out her cigarette in the metal ashtray on the table. "No, the only thing I'm interested in is money."

Which was a lie, because she was also interested in political issues, but that was fine. "I'm looking for a server address."

"For?"

"Genovary."

Incache scowled. "Those bastards. Word on the street is that they're up to no good at all."

"That's my belief as well. Genetic manipulation, I hear."

The other woman nodded sharply. "That's close enough to the rumors I've heard. Usual price."

"Of course." That would be both a money transfer and a favor owed. Didn't matter. The one she could handle now, and the other was a future problem.

Incache handed over a card. "Good luck."

Nakano nodded. "Thanks. I'm afraid I'll need it."

CHAPTER TWENTY-FIVE

Nakano dropped out of the magical dark web's sky at the address Incache had provided. She had expected to see a high-tech building. Instead, it was a dilapidated hospital. Her mind automatically calculated the time period of the place, as it always did, but she couldn't get any more precise than 1800s America.

She had landed far enough back to be in the grass circle in the center of a small cobblestone road. Around her, weeds and scrub filled lawns that had probably once been manicured. High trees with gnarled branches cast strange, twisted shadows in the moonlight. A wrought iron fence guarded the perimeter, but sections had fallen away, and several of the spear points at the top had bent or broken. She turned to examine it all around and noticed that the main gate hung on broken hinges.

As she turned back toward the entrance, she noted the breeze playing with the debris on the grounds. It was definitely an image, somewhere between a Halloween comedy and a legit horror film.

The building loomed against the dark sky. Soot and grime irregularly darkened the red bricks making up its façade. It rose to four stories with a steep roof above. A central tower positioned over the double doors that were the building's main entrance extended an additional story and a half. The gargoyle on top peered down as if judging her for thinking of entering.

The top three floors had identical windows, each a regularly spaced tall rectangle. Most were fitted with iron bars, and she wondered if that was to keep people out or to keep people in. There were fewer windows on the bottom floor, and they, too, were a mix of bars and not. None permitted her to see inside.

She watched her steps carefully as she climbed the crumbling stone steps toward the entrance. The massive oak doors were closed and flanked by columns that didn't look any sturdier than the stairs. Above the entrance, carved into the stone, was the hospital's name. Angelic Heights.

Nakano was pushed gently aside from behind as data walked past her and through the doors to enter the server. She wondered where the data had been before that. Usually, it was present from the moment she arrived. Perhaps the whole view so far had been like a cutscene in a video game, a chance for her to appreciate the ambiance before getting into the details.

The data resembled patients moving in ones, twos, or threes, some with bandages, others with open wounds. With a grimace, she modified her avatar to look like them and followed them inside, walking through the still-closed doors like they did.

The authenticity of the exterior carried on as she stepped inside. Even before her eyes took in the place, the smells of acid, soap, and something else that reminded her of decay assaulted her nostrils. She dampened her sense of smell, thankful that such things were possible in the simulation, and stared out at the large room.

Gas lamps mounted on wrought iron brackets on the walls provided flickering illumination, revealing the simulated misery of the occupants. Patients sat in chairs to the left and right, waiting for attention. More stood near the reception desk.

Three doors led from the room. The one to the left was marked Administration, the one ahead was Emergency, and the one to the right was Medical. A carpet runner that had probably once been a cheery shade of red was positioned along the path to each, a poor choice for a hospital, she thought. They were dingy and stained with age. The walls were covered in wood to the midway point, then painted an institutional green that looked gross.

Nakano instructed her system to take pictures because when she told the others about this, it would be necessary for them to see it for themselves. For a modern pharmaceutical company to represent itself this way struck her as particularly sick and twisted. She thought maybe that pointed to the research they were doing, as well.

She limped toward the door labeled Administration. Two hulking orderlies stood in front of it, clad in dingy white tunics over dingy white trousers and black boots scuffed with age. One stared at her, while the other instructed politely enough, "Patients don't go this way. Check the desk."

She turned awkwardly and complied. A woman behind the desk wore a similar outfit, but with a white hat over her brunette curls. She gave Nakano an evil smile. "Leg problem, huh? Second floor. Enjoy the stairs."

Nakano ignored the itch in her hand that wanted to draw her katana and lop the woman's head off and headed for the staircase instead. At the top, she discovered a waiting room similar to the one below and a closed door. She didn't have time to wait, so when the next piece of data went through, she pretended to be with them. The nurse behind the desk was frazzled and bored, and there was no other security, so no one tried to stop her.

A long hallway stretched into the distance, seemingly extending for the full length of the hospital. It was lined with symmetrical doors, several of which were open. She looked inside as she passed and saw iron beds with thin, stained mattresses covered by heavy, stained blankets. A small table with a basin was beside each, and in storage beneath it she saw old bottles with handwritten labels. The windows let in hardly any light, making the room entirely dingy.

In another room, she noted that wire mesh covered the window in addition to the bars. She wondered if it was to prevent an escape attempt. The next door she came to was locked, but she peered through the small sliding metal window to see a cell with padded walls and floor. She hadn't considered that the hospital might be a place for the mentally ill as well, and the inclusion turned her stomach even more.

She was almost overjoyed when she found a room that wasn't entirely depressing. It was a staff room with lockers, tables, counters, and chairs. A strange metal object that her system informed her was a speaking tube graced one wall. She had never seen one. It seemed to vibrate with the sound of creepy whispers, and she steadfastly ignored it.

Most importantly, a wall held framed layouts of each level of the hospital. She noted a single unmarked spot on each floor that appeared to be in a diagonal line from top to bottom, which struck her as suspicious. It was a few moments' work to locate it, and she opened a nondescript door, marked Janitorial, to find a steep staircase. "Now we're talking."

She took the stairs carefully. Every second or third step creaked underneath her like it would break, but she reached the bottom without incident, keenly aware that she was now underground. A short hallway led to a massive iron door with rivets. Two orderlies stood there, but unlike the ones above, they held black nightsticks in their hands. At the sight of her, they started slapping the weapons into their open palms in a strangely synchronized display of aggression.

Nakano smiled, reached into her tunic, grabbed two of the grenades from her belt, and tossed them at the orderlies. They surged forward, but not before the small containers exploded with a hiss of gas. Both fell but didn't pixel away. She couldn't leave them behind her, so she discarded her disguise, drew her sword, and stabbed each.

Neither of the bodies left a key for the door behind when they vanished, so she pulled her lockpick set from her gauntlet and applied the picks to the door. When the tumblers clicked, she stood, drew her sword again, and readied herself for what might be beyond it. As she yanked the door open, the sensory power of the place assaulted her again, and she paused to push her instinctive reactions down.

The corridor was as long as the one above had been. Gas lamps flickered at irregular intervals, many of them extinguished, and cast pools of shadow along the hallway. The smell of decay warred with astringent chemicals, and worst of all, moans and screams at different volumes came from everywhere.

Nakano muttered, "Nice ambiance, scumbags. I should publish this on the web, so everyone sees how sick you are." She activated a recording, thinking maybe she would, depending on how things worked out, then stomped down the hallway, ready to deliver some severe damage to people who had earned it.

CHAPTER TWENTY-SIX

Nakano moved cautiously down the corridor. Like the hospital floor she'd visited above, this one had doors that mirrored one another on opposite sides, although the placement suggested the rooms beyond them were larger. A sign sticking out from the wall above each door declared the room to be Surgery with a number after it, and a sign hanging from the ceiling proclaimed that the whole hallway belonged to Surgery. Screams, shouts, moans, and pleading came through the thin wood of the doors. Again, she shook her head at the choice of simulation and mumbled, "Whoever did this, you are one sick puppy."

The sounds were bait to draw an invader into a defended position. She had broken into too many servers to be caught by something that simple, but it was still enough to set her nerves on edge, cause her teeth to itch, and make her hands clench.

She drew her katana and continued moving forward, activating an enhanced sight mode that allowed her to see behind her at the cost of some distortion to her vision ahead. She would accept the tradeoff. If something came through one of the doors, she wanted to know about it. Each step she took seemed to transform the hallway ahead, making it cleaner, sharper in resolution, and less like a horror video game.

The corridor made a right-angle turn ahead, and a sign at the junction proclaimed, Research. Her initial reaction was to prefer that option to Surgery, but given the twisted nature of the place, she wasn't sure that was a logical assumption. Since it was the *only* option, she took the turn cautiously, ready to fight.

The corridor went fifteen feet, then turned again. That arrangement felt like a deliberate setup, and she moved even more carefully toward the corner and deployed her small analysis device to peer around the bend.

The hallway was a mirror to the one she'd been in except for the rather more elegant door at the far end and the four orderlies who stood near it, two with their backs against each flanking wall. She drew back her device and readied herself for a fight. She sheathed her sword and filled both hands with grenades, a combination of gas, smoke, and ones that discharged tiny flechettes.

If these were low-level bots, the grenades would probably be sufficient to take them out. If her foes were medium level or higher, the grenades would provide a distraction that would allow her to close. Depending on what weapons they were hiding or what traps might lie along it, the hallway was a perfect killing ground. She needed to create an advantage for herself.

Nakano dispatched the analysis drone again as she

dashed around the corner. She needed to cover a minimum of fifteen feet before she could be assured of the throw getting to where it needed to go. In those fifteen feet, she jumped over one tripwire, slid under a detection beam on her knees with her shoulders back against the floor, then threw herself into a forward somersault to avoid a pressure plate. She came up running, which was good, because she had landed on another plate. Wicked barbed darts shot across behind her, and several scraped against her armor.

She threw the grenades, then drew her sword as she snapped the verbal command to activate her cloak, which swirled around her and changed color to match the smoke that was billowing into the corridor. The guards had reacted before she threw the grenades, with two charging at her and two staying by the door. All pulled menacing hand weapons from behind their backs.

The first pair emerged from the smoke but didn't see her immediately thanks to her cloak's camouflage. They didn't realize she was there until she was between them and a horizontal strike with her sword to the one on the right lopped his head off. Both skull and body pixelated into nothingness as she threw a back fist at the orderly on her left. He dove forward to avoid it and rolled to his feet gripping a wicked-looking piece of wood with spikes sticking out of it. If anyone made a movie about a murderous baseball player, he would be a shoo-in for the starring role.

He whipped the spiked club at her in a diagonal strike. She slashed her katana across on an intersecting path to meet it, confident her blade would chop his weapon in two. The shock of impact matched the mental shock as it sank in and got stuck in the wood. The downward momentum of his strike twisted her sideways as it pulled the weapon from her hands. She continued the motion into a spin and cross-drew the throwing knives in her forearm sheaths. She ended the move by dropping down low and stabbing both at his left leg. He raised his foot to block and stopped one, but the other plunged through his boot and into the side of his foot.

He howled and brought the spiked club down in a frenzied strike. The blow would have ended her had she not swept up her cloak, wrapped the weapon in it, and thrown herself backward. He didn't release his grip on the club and stumbled forward as a result.

She pulled her legs up to her chest and kicked out with both heels, smashing them into his knees. He bellowed in rage as the joints bent in the wrong direction, then he dropped to his side on the floor. She grabbed a flechette grenade from her belt, slapped it on the back of his head, and held him at arm's length. His skull prevented any shards from reaching her as it detonated, then he vanished into nothingness. His weapon disappeared with him.

Nakano's cloak healed itself as she rose. She extended a hand, and the magnet in her gauntlet connected to the magnet in her sword and brought it to her grip as the other two orderlies appeared from the smoke, coming to check on their allies. This pair carried odd-looking pistols that were far larger than usual and had a strangely rectangular and boxy design. She found out why as they spat streams of bullets at her.

She rushed forward while spinning the cloak around her. Bullets deflected from it when the edge connected with them but punched through other parts of the fabric to slam into her armor. She snapped the command to extrude the face mask from the helmet as the barrage continued.

The defensive efforts bought her enough time to reach them, although she took wounds in her left arm and right shoulder along the way. The injuries degraded her capabilities by slowing her actions but weren't enough to stop her as she engaged the enemy on her left.

With that hand, she slapped the bot's weapon toward the floor, then delivered a wicked high kick with her left foot toward his head. Halfway there, she gave the mental command to extend the spike in the toe, a nasty trick both her avatars possessed. He got a hand up to block, but the spike stabbed through his hand and into his head. He didn't pixelate away, which proved equal parts fortunate and unfortunate.

As he fell, he pulled her from her feet and dropped her hard on the floor. The impact reverberated through her body as she struck the hard tiles. The move carried her out of the path of the other one's bullets, and his gun clicked empty before he could adjust to her new position.

Nakano managed a weak strike with her katana from her awkward position, and the keen blade sliced into the standing man's shin and broke the bone. He joined them on the floor, and she pulled the weapon back and stabbed him in the chest with it, transfixing his heart. A blow smashed onto the armor on her back as he pixelated away, signaling that the one she'd kicked in the head was still among the living. She wrenched her body to yank the spike free, then kicked immediately back again. This time his block failed, and he vanished in a glitter of computer code.

She slowly climbed to her feet, feeling battered. She initiated a self-check and repair, waiting as her systems pulled resources from pristine routines to bolster those that had been damaged. Given enough time, she could heal completely here, but she doubted she would have such a luxury, and instead pulled the medkit from her gauntlet. It held bandages, which she didn't need, and an almost cartoonishly huge syringe she did.

Nakano stabbed it through the fabric into her thigh and pushed the plunger down. Icy cold energy flowed through her, a temporary boost that would last her ten minutes at most and leave her crashed afterward. She had to find what she sought in that interval or log out and try again. The latter would be impossible since the company's security response would be on alert for longer than she would be able to wait for the information.

She retrieved one of her fallen throwing knives to hold in her off hand and stomped toward the door at the end of the corridor. She ran forward, leapt, and landed a booted foot on the lock. The door exploded open, and she stepped through the opening, primed to fight.

She had expected a lab, or maybe a morgue, but what she entered was an operating theater being used as a classroom. Two-thirds of the circular space was occupied by students sitting in tiers on benches, each of them with a clear view of the central area.

In that space, a surgeon and a nurse stood over a

patient who lay on a gurney. A large drill was positioned at the man's skull as if ready to crack it open, and both the surgeon and nurse held evil-looking operating instruments.

Nakano called, "Uh, hi there. Is this Biology 101?"

They attacked.

CHAPTER TWENTY-SEVEN

Nakano had had enough. The entire simulation had made her angry. The not-so-subtle emotional manipulations were a constant jangle against her nerves. These two had to be infomancers, and one of them had probably designed this place. It was beyond time to take out the trash.

The surgeon approached her from ahead, and the nurse diagonally from the right. The former gripped a massive bone saw in both hands while the latter only carried a scalpel, so moving to the right seemed like the logical choice. Nakano shifted, careful not to move too far back where the audience could get hold of her. So far, they hadn't reacted other than with noise, but she would be hard-pressed to survive if they were part of the system's defenses.

She managed to get the nurse between herself and the doctor, taking only a slash against the armor from the scalpel as payment. Her sword whipped around at the other woman's head, but the nurse evaded it, ducking as it went by, then popping back up to slash at her hand. The scalpel struck sparks off her gauntlet.

Nakano growled, "All right, enough of this garbage." She whipped her off hand behind her back and drew the pistol. She had aimed it at the nurse's forehead when the patient kicked her hand and knocked the gun out of line, sending the bullet into the doorframe.

Nakano spun away from the patient and the nurse but ended up a foot away from the audience with nowhere to go and a pair of enemies closing in. She let her right leg collapse and rolled on her shoulders, an awkward move that nonetheless kept her away from her enemies and the crowd. She popped up and pulled the trigger at the nurse, but the patient threw himself in the way. He absorbed three bullets, then fell against her and yanked the gun out of her hand as he fell and pixelated away.

There was no time to retrieve the gun. She whipped her sword around in time to intercept the bone saw as it slashed down at her, and the two weapons ground against each other with a hiss and shriek of tortured metal. She snapped a front kick that knocked the surgeon back, then tried a lunge to stab him through the stomach. He blocked it with the bone saw, then grinned. "Do you like our little simulation?"

Nakano recognized it as the distraction it was and retracted the sword, lifted its pommel high, then blindly stabbed backward. The blade pierced the nurse through the solar plexus, and she pixelated away as her scalpel fell with a clatter. Nakano grinned at the surgeon arrogantly. "Love it. You'll make a fantastic ghost to inhabit it, I think."

She brought the blade around with a flourish to block his next attack with the large saw.

He didn't seem impressed. "Or I'll come find you in the real world, and we'll try a little surgery there." Taunts like that always made her check her back trace, and she discovered the server had launched a bot to follow her signal. It wasn't far along and wasn't moving fast enough to reach her before she logged out, so she dismissed it from her mind and focused on the man in front of her.

When he swung the bone saw again, she feigned a block, then slid her sword under his weapon. He overcompensated as his weapon swung past the expected contact point, and she slashed him on the outside of his right arm, near the shoulder. She brought up her knee in a strike to his solar plexus and he grunted as the air left his body.

Before she could reverse her blade and swipe at him again, he grabbed a nearby tray of implements and hurled its contents at her. Scalpels of every size sped toward her like an expert had thrown them. She blocked several with her blade, but three sank into her flesh, and another sliced a cut in her cheek.

She pulled them out one by one and tossed them on the floor as he dropped the saw and flicked his wrists. Two daggers appeared in them, looking not even remotely like surgical implements. She observed, "Cheap tricks by a cheap trickster."

"Says the samurai carrying a gun."

"Touché."

His dual weapons forced her onto the defensive, blocking strike after strike with deft twists of her sword but unable to counter. He pressed her steadily backward and followed her around the room as she tried to evade, attempting to herd her. She didn't know where to but was sure she didn't want to find out. She was reluctant to throw away one of her best tools, but two infomancers in the same place usually meant she had reached the end of the run, so she ripped her cloak from her shoulders and threw it at him.

He attempted to knock it aside, but the cloak grabbed him and wrapped around his arms, binding them together. It had a limited AI to fight on its own and resisted his efforts to break free. She ran forward, leaving herself wide open to do it since his arms were busy, and stabbed her katana at his heart. His blades cut through the cloak and moved to block, but got there an instant too late. They rang against her metal after it had sunk into his flesh.

He looked at her wide-eyed for a moment, then pixelated away.

Nakano panted as she waited for the information she sought to make itself known, but it didn't. She scowled at the gurney, which had fallen over, at the strewn medical implements on the floor, and the remains of her cloak. She would have searched the body, but none had been left behind. The prize wouldn't be in the crowd, would it? Doubtful.

She lifted her gun from the floor, discovered that it had been damaged during the fight, and shoved the useless weapon back in her belt. She slipped her throwing knife back into her gauntlet and reached for one of the scalpels to use as an off hand blade. It vanished as she touched it, and she cursed loudly. Whoever had coded this place had done it well.

She stared around the room, shifting through visual modes, and finally spotted a glass pane on the wall beyond the top row of students. So, more challenges awaited her. Nakano steeled herself as she assessed the situation. The only way to reach it was by going up through the ranks of the watching students, and if they decided to attack her, things would be bad.

Thinking about it for too long would be bad as well, so she gripped her sword in her right hand, readied herself, and leapt to the first railing. From there she jumped from railing to railing in a long-strided run, avoiding contact with the crowd, which ignored her. She curled up on her final leap, which carried her through the glass. It shattered all around her, and she landed in a crouch.

The room beyond was unexpectedly large, and a single man stood inside, surrounded by chalkboards with strange symbols drawn on them. He was tall, with sandy brown hair, a clipped mustache and beard, round spectacles atop an undistinguished nose, and wore a suit underneath a white lab coat with a caduceus symbol on it. One hand held a pen, and the other grasped a clipboard.

He nodded at her. "Well done, you, taking out my students so adroitly."

"You mean the surgeon and the nurse."

"New to infomancy, well, relatively speaking. Newer than you or me, for certain."

Nakano held her sword in a defensive posture. "And you are?"

He smiled. "The one who will defeat you and kick you out of my server."

"With your pen and your clipboard?"

He rewarded the comment with a thin smile. "With my pen and my clipboard." He attacked on the last word, and she barely got her sword twisted around in time to intercept the pen that plunged toward her jugular vein. She took a blow from the clipboard on her ribs and felt one of them break under the impact. She backpedaled, trying to get some space to work with, but he moved with her, almost skin to skin. The pen stabbed down into her leg, a blow she accepted to gain an opportunity for a counterattack, but his clipboard intercepted her sword stroke, and she had to release the pommel with her left hand to get her gauntlet up in time to intercept the pen as it came at her neck again.

His moves were so fast they were blurs in her vision, but his face was peaceful, as if it wasn't involved in the fight. She hated him, hated the server, and decided she hated the company too, for good measure. Finally, she hated the only option she could see that might defeat him, but since it was the only one, she tried it anyway.

She stepped forward and slashed down with the katana, and when he blocked it with the clipboard, she let the sword fly free from her hand. The arm that had held it moved up and over his shoulder as the other shifted under his other arm. The cost for the latter was a deep stab from the pen into her shoulder.

Nakano had both hands behind his back, and her chest was fully in contact with his as she drove him backward. She pulled the throwing knife from its forearm sheath and positioned it properly as her legs continued to propel them both. The pen stabbed into the back of her shoulder repeatedly, causing her left arm to fall limp, but it didn't matter. Only the right one did, the one that held the blade.

The clipboard savaged her ribs as he repeatedly smashed it into her, breaking more of them, but then she slammed him against the wall with her body against his. The impact drove his neck back onto her knife blade, the handle held firm by the wall. His eyes widened, then he coughed and collapsed to his knees. He pixelated away slowly as if still stunned by what she had done, even now not believing it was possible.

His fallen clipboard changed color, and she picked it up with her working hand to see that papers had appeared on it, the notes she needed. She shoved it under her useless arm, retrieved her katana, sheathed it, and logged out, knowing she would have to spend some serious time coding before she could deploy as Nakano again, but judging the result worth the cost.

CHAPTER TWENTY-EIGHT

When Billie arrived the next day, Izzy was waiting for her. The infomancer shared the information she had found the night before, and Billie set the wheels in motion. An hour later, the team was seated in the conference room, and the Spellbound crew was present on the wall display. No doubt her team showed likewise at their place.

Billie stated, "You should all listen to what Izzy has to say."

Izzy looked like she hadn't slept all night because she had spent those hours breaking the seal on the data she'd retrieved. "It looks like a race to create supersoldiers. Actually, I don't know if we can really call it a race. Spellbound's CEO client's company, Cellgeniks, is further ahead than Genovary."

Caleb replied, "Which would give them a reason to cheat."

"True. And to cut corners. Cellgeniks is taking a more standard course, using gene therapies to modify humans and magicals in small ways. Kind of a continuation of what's been done in the past."

Danica muttered, "Always searching for the supersoldier." Her tone suggested she didn't support the idea much.

Izzy replied, "Exactly. Genovary seems more interested in seeing what they can get than any rigorous research process. It seems like they're throwing things at the wall, charting the results, and hoping it will lead somewhere."

Eileen asked, "Has it led anywhere yet?" Her interest in the research on the topic was clear in her tone.

"I found records mentioning elementals, but nothing consistent. There's a mountain of stuff in the file, and it's not logically collected. If I had to guess, I found my way into a data trash bin that hadn't been emptied yet or hadn't been emptied well."

Anya asked, "Elemental, as in fire dude?"

Billie interjected, "I was thinking that myself."

Izzy shrugged. "I don't know. I went through a lot to get this apparently trashed data, so I have no idea what kind of stuff they might have had better protected."

Billie replied, "This is certainly something the Magical Threats division needs to address. I'll make sure those above me are in the know. But that doesn't solve Spellbound's immediate problem if this company is actually after their client, directly or through intermediaries."

Danica added, "If anything, this revelation makes it worse. We have a gig coming up that I wasn't worried about before, but that I'm seriously worried about now. There's a huge convention center on the river here in Cleveland, and our CEO client is speaking to a leadership seminar being held there Thursday night."

Caleb asked, "You couldn't talk him out of it?"

Danica shook her head. "No. It's a thing he's done for decades now. He won't be moved."

Anya asked, "Additional security?"

Alex replied, "The venue has enhanced security on site. We'll be there, some in gear, some in street clothes, and additional infomancers will be tied in to watch over things."

Danica interrupted, "But it would be really good to have you there, I think."

It was an easy decision for Billie. "We're in, assuming we get the go-ahead from above."

"Thanks. Really. I mean it. We'll send over all the data we have. We'll start revising our planning based on this new information as soon as we're off the call." The Spellbound team logged out a few minutes later, leaving Voltaic behind to listen in and coordinate.

Caleb observed, "The coincidence here is too convenient by far for it to be random."

Billie nodded. "Agreed. The likelihood of a strike at the event is, like, a thousand percent."

Izzy asked, "Should we pull in CIR?"

"I'd say having them standing by isn't a terrible idea. They could be a perimeter guard to watch over the building."

Caleb replied, "Agree."

"I'll run that up through channels too, but I'm sure Helen will give the okay to both our involvement and theirs as long as nothing blows up here."

Onyx interjected, "Keeping my fingers and toes crossed."

The others laughed, but everyone with the possible exception of the pixie had their minds focused on the task ahead.

The intervening hours from Tuesday morning to Thursday afternoon passed quickly, lost in a haze of preparations and logistics. The others were hanging around on the equipment floor when Billie and Caleb walked by on the way to gear up. Their new armor was waiting in their lockers, and Billie waved the left arm around as she climbed into her armor, again testing the unfamiliar weight of the collapsible shield positioned there.

She noted the others doing the same and was sure that like her, each of them wanted to deploy it to ensure it worked. Eileen had warned against that because of the power required to deploy and retract the object, so she resisted, as did they. As Billie slid into her top and fastened it, she noted an additional ammunition holder, sized for the little micro-grenade rectangles that would attach to the pistols in the other room.

Billie headed there, found hers, and slid it into the modified holster on the equipment belt. She added two reloads for the rifle, one for the pistol, and a micro-grenade block to the slots in the chest armor, then selected a full complement of nonlethal grenades. There was no telling what might happen tonight, but it was almost certain that innocents would be around for it. She warned the others to do the same as they joined her.

After he was fully geared up, Caleb shrugged like he was donning a heavy weight. "Gear's getting bulky."

Onyx was beside Billie. She retorted, "Be stronger. Be faster. Be better."

He countered, "Not all of us have magic that allows us to hide from the fight like you."

She gestured with her bow. "Would you like an arrow in the neck?"

He laughed. "I think I'll pass."

Anya entered the room wearing the same armor as the rest of them. Stealth wasn't an issue, so she had chosen to go with the version that offered the expanding shield.

Billie asked, "Are you thinking of adding the shield to your other armor?"

The scout shook her head. "Too heavy and bulky."

Caleb needled, "See? I'm not the only one."

Onyx mimed pulling her bowstring, and Billie muttered, "Hush." To Anya, she continued, "Makes sense."

Quentin walked in, carrying the case that held his long rifle.

Anya asked, "Happy to finally be sniping, Cueball?"

He chuckled. "Sure, although you'll probably wind up having all the fun in the building while I lie outside and bake on the rooftop."

"You chose this life."

"It's what I'm best at, that's true."

Billie looked around. Everyone was ready. "Enough chatting. Let's move." She had visited the place on the previous day, so she opened a portal outside the anti-magic zone between the building and the river. They all walked through, and she let the portal fall behind them.

Caleb observed, "With the street closed, this makes a great landing area."

Billie replied, "Yeah, be sure to spike it with some cameras. A lot of cameras."

Over the comm, Izzy replied, "I have a plan for the camera placement, never fear. We'll have eyes everywhere."

Caleb asked, "How many drones are you bringing, Z?"

"Three, all combat."

"So you're a little worried, too."

"No, I'm a lot worried. If you could have seen that server, you'd understand. These are some sick freaks."

Billie replied, "All the more reason for us to stay focused. We'll operate in teams as discussed. Caleb, Prem, and Deacon, you're one group. Onyx, Anya, and Hannah will be with me. Izzy, when we need to hear from the other team, you'll have us looped in, right?"

"You know it, boss. Everything on my end is ready to go. After Eileen gets back from delivering the SUV to you, she'll help out with the drones."

"All right. Caleb, you and your people help get Izzy's stuff into place. Quentin, up to the roof, same deal. Onyx, Anya, Hannah, and I will do the interior sweep. Move, people."

Billie walked through the venue, trying to see it again with new eyes. She had been through the day before to match up what she'd seen on the blueprints with the real-world equivalents and had recorded it for everyone else. The main exhibition floor was closed during the event, and security would be watching it carefully. Her team's focus was the small arena that hosted music, theater, and motivational speakers.

The floor and tiered seats were all in place around the centrally located oval stage, and the technicians were running through calibration tests on the video screens overhead that faced in all four directions as they walked in.

The setup looked like a rock concert rather than a leadership conference, and she said so.

Anya replied, "Probably costs a lot more for this show, though."

Onyx quipped, "And a rock show would probably be less likely to be attacked."

Hannah drew heavy-duty scanners from the duffels she carried and handed them out. They worked in a pattern, running the sensors along the seats, the stage, and even the walls and floors. Then they moved out of the room and repeated the process, radiating outward from the venue until they had covered all the spaces they logically could. The search took an hour and a half, and they finished it at a small snack bar, drinking sodas to refresh themselves.

Izzy reported, "Nothing on the scans. Looking good."

Billie replied, "Excellent. Give us ten minutes to recover, then tell them to kill the anti-magic emitters. We'll make the sweep as fast as we can."

The anti-magic emitters dropped at the appointed time, and they redid the walk with Billie, Anya, and Hannah using their magical abilities to search for trouble. Once again, they came up with nothing.

Billie instructed, "All right, kick it back on again. Whatever they're gonna do, it's either amazingly well-hidden or not here yet."

Over the comm, Caleb offered, "Or nothing's going to happen."

Izzy laughed. "Yeah, right. You just keep thinking that and maybe it'll come true, like any other fairy tale."

Billie prompted, "Okay, folks. Get what rest you can. We'll need game faces on in sixty minutes."

CHAPTER TWENTY-NINE

Onyx and Billie were in the performance area when the time came for things to kick into gear. Above them, Jilly zipped around, checking things from the air and searching for a perch on the video boards.

Billie commented, "I love that little dragon."

Onyx replied, "Me too." She looked up and tapped her black-painted fingernails on her chin. "You know, if I shrank down small enough, I could probably ride on the dragon. That would be fun."

Billie chuckled. "I'm sure she would think so, too."

"Maybe another time."

Camera feeds appeared in her lens as Billie moved toward her position in the hallway between the performance arena and the space for the meet-and-greet session. Izzy was keeping their visual fields fairly uncluttered but had provided two important windows.

One showed the front of the convention center as a motorcade pulled up. Police motorcycles flanked the three-car convoy, and a man who very much resembled the CEO of Cellgeniks climbed from the back of the first. He waved at the sign-carrying protesters who shouted things at him from behind the barricades, lifted a hand to his ear to suggest he couldn't hear them, and walked inside.

It was a tense moment for her people and the Spellbound team because while all that was going on out front and potentially attracting trouble, the real CEO had walked out of a portal near where Billie and her team had arrived. The Spellbound crew bustled him inside, and everyone let out a simultaneous sigh of relief when he was safely within the convention center's walls.

Izzy commented, "That's one challenge out of the way."

Caleb replied, "Well, he should be safe for the next ninety minutes, until the event starts."

Onyx countered, "Unless someone in the meet-and-greet tries to kill him."

Billie gently slapped the pixie on the shoulder with the back of her hand. "Always thinking on the bright side, aren't you?"

Anya countered, "She's just stressed because we're on the outside where we can't help protect him."

"Yeah, me too."

Izzy added windows to their displays, showing the camera feeds from inside the meet-and-greet room. The CEO had brought a pair of his regular bodyguards, a man and a woman in dark suits who stayed at his sides. Several Spellbound people, including Danica, were in the room dressed in street clothes.

After a moment, Izzy's system began applying designators to the people in the room. The Spellbound Security members were outlined in yellow, and a number of other undercover security people, presumably from the venue, were outlined in orange. The infomancer gave them an aerial view from the drone. Quentin had a green outline on the roof, and several positions on the perimeter where clusters of CIR people stood had blue outlines in Billie's vision. Everything looked fine.

Deacon complained, "I could have been in the room. I would fit right in among the billionaire crowd, I'm sure of it."

Anya asked, "Have you done it before, Preacher?"

"Millionaires, yes. Haven't cracked that stratospheric height of the extra zeroes yet."

Prem asked, "Any good investment advice?"

Their infiltration expert laughed. "Tons, but with what we get paid, who has money left to invest?"

Onyx beat everyone else to the reply. "Have Z embezzle you some."

Izzy replied, "I'm busy embezzling for myself at the moment, thanks, but I'd be willing to do it for a significant share of the profits, say seventy percent."

The banter continued until the doors opened to the public and people began funneling into the performance space. Then everyone's attention stayed locked on the cameras, the detectors, and the security positions.

Billie and Onyx remained in the hallway that connected the green room and the meet-and-greet area to the performance space. Anya and Hannah were nearby in an intersecting corridor. Caleb's team was already in the arena, positioned around the room.

The less impressive speakers were in the green room

awaiting the notice to move. All seemed to be as it should be. Now and again, Izzy reported that her AIs saw nothing out of the ordinary. Voltaic maintained communication with all of them, requiring confirmation from each checkpoint at ten-minute intervals.

Billie did her best to stay calm and relaxed while she waited. She mused inwardly once again that she couldn't do what Danica and her team did. The constant stress of it would make her nuts.

Finally, the time came. Danica advised, "Moving to the arena now."

Billie and Onyx stood straighter, and Billie knew the rest of her team would be doing the same. As the Spellbound team left the meet-and-greet room, several reported they were moving away to put on armor. Danica and Alex stayed with the principal, offering tense smiles as they walked past.

Billie and Onyx followed, and when they were inside the arena, Danica reported, "Jilly says everything looks good from overhead."

Applause began as the crowd saw the speakers. They bounded up to the stage accompanied by flashing lights and blaring music. Moments of change like this were always prime times for an attack, but the show got underway without any sign of danger. It was almost possible to believe the night would end without an attack. *A pleasant fairy tale.* Billie remembered Onyx's earlier comment.

Billie stood in an aisle near the stage with her rifle pointing toward the floor. The crowd had been warned that security would be present, and if her martial appearance concerned anyone around her, they didn't show it.

The first sign of trouble arrived twenty-five minutes into the program. Izzy warned, "Someone is attacking the venue's security server. The best I can say right now is whoever's doing it isn't an amateur."

Danica replied, "Prep for evac, but no one moves yet."

A minute later, Quentin reported, "I've got heavy SUVs inbound from all directions."

Camera windows flicked up to show the feeds from all sides of the building. Izzy replied, "Looks coordinated. Drones are ready to respond."

Billie asked, "Cueball, can you stop them without hurting them?"

"As long as you're fine with me hurting the vehicles."

"How sure are you that they're bad guys?"

"I'm not. Fifty-fifty at best."

That wasn't the answer Billie wanted to hear. "Hell. Wait until that's at least seventy-five twenty-five, then you're free to engage. Again, limit damage to objects, not people, as best you can."

"Got it, Basher."

Izzy advised, "I'm bringing two drones down to defend the other directions and leaving one up on overwatch."

Voltaic added, "My drones are on their way to scan the vehicles. Maybe we'll get some useful information."

Billie activated a private channel to Danica. "You sure on that hold?"

"It would be an embarrassment to rush him out of here."

"I'd be bad at working for clients, because that's not a thing I would even think to care about."

Danica chuckled darkly. "Trust me, I'm not all that great at it either."

Billie watched the video as the SUVs sped toward the convention center, then pulled up simultaneously. As the doors opened, Quentin announced, "People with guns piling out of the SUVs on three sides of the building."

Danica asked, "Which way is clear?"

Voltaic replied, "The water side. Local PD still has that road locked down."

A shout of alarm caused Billie's head to snap around. Several people in the crowd were moving as others near them scrambled to get out of the way. Blood flew, the smell of it instantly recognizable. The people who were fighting toward the stage had thin rods of plastic in their hands that had obviously been ground down to a point. She had no idea how they got the improvised weapons in, but that wasn't relevant at the moment.

Danica snapped, "All right, people. We're busted. Evac now. Jilly, clear out this trash."

Billie and Onyx ran toward the nearest exit. Their role in an evacuation was to control the corridor outside the performance arena. They smashed through the door with the pixie in the lead and Billie following with her rifle up. No enemies were present, and a path toward the egress nearest the street protected by the police appeared in their display. When Danica and the close protection team exited the arena, Billie and Onyx moved ahead along the path to safety.

The comms were alive with information. Quentin warned that several had made it inside from the west. Other members of her team reported in as they moved to secure their areas of responsibility for an escape toward the river. The infomancers reported on their efforts to deal with the new arrivals.

Billie and Onyx had almost reached the exit doors when the invaders reached them. A group of four people with guns appeared unexpectedly from the left, slamming open the doors that led to the catering area and surging through. Billie barked the command to deploy her bullet-proof shield and crouched behind it as Onyx moved behind her. Bullets slammed into it but didn't hit her. She warned, "Contact."

Danica asked, "Reroute?"

"No, give us a sec." She drew her pistol, angled it up, switched to micro grenades, and pulled the trigger four times. As with her physical grenades, she had chosen all flash-bangs because she wanted to avoid damage to innocents. They went off almost simultaneously, and the incoming fire slackened. She switched the pistol back to bullets, leaned around the shield, and delivered triple taps to each of the four attackers, dropping them.

Billie stood, retracted the shield, and changed magazines in the pistol while Onyx aimed an arrow in the general direction of their fallen foes. Billie advised, "They're down. Looks like they'll stay down. Come through."

She holstered the pistol and pointed her rifle at them. None moved, and Danica and her client passed safely through the area. Billie followed when the protectors were out of the way and ran with Danica for the edge of the anti-magic field. She almost groaned in pleasure as the stifling weight of the anti-magic field faded away.

Before anyone could open a portal, a familiar figure appeared ahead, already throwing a wash of flame at them.

CHAPTER THIRTY

Billie was moving before her mind had fully processed the situation. She wrapped force shields around herself and everyone nearby and placed another wall of force in between her and Fire Guy, which was what she'd taken to calling him in her mind. She lifted her rifle and fired at his face as she cautiously advanced. The bullets evaporated as they hit the shields of fire wrapped around him. He gave no indication of being bothered by them. She snarled a curse.

Onyx snapped, "I need high ground."

Billie hadn't realized the pixie was still beside her. She dropped the rifle to dangle on its strap and gestured to send the pixie, who was already crouched and ready for the move, flying on a disk of force magic up toward the balcony that ran around the convention center's second level. She nudged the trajectory to ensure Onyx would land safely, then returned her attention to Fire Guy, trusting the pixie to handle her descent.

Pressure in her mind caused her to reach for Dorian,

and she drew the blade in her off hand as she simultaneously yanked her pistol from its holster. The bullets from the pistol had no greater effect than the rounds from the rifle had, so she shoved it back into its holster.

The grenades she was carrying wouldn't be any good against this enemy, and she had forgotten to switch out the micro-grenade launcher. She wished she had a frost grenade, wondered if such things existed, then forgot about it as she stared at Fire Guy, wondering what the hell she could do to hurt him.

Danica warned, "We have to get our principal to safety, but Jilly's staying to help. You won't be able to talk to her, so trust she'll be here to cause trouble. For the bad guys, mostly."

Billie cast frost magic through both Dorian and her open hand, but even that wasn't adequate to quench the flames. They would stutter where she held the beam but not go away entirely.

The monster flinched as the bark of a sniper rifle sounded in the distance. Quentin had aimed at the hole she was making in its defenses, but even the huge bullet from his firearm hadn't gotten through enough to damage the thing.

She cursed, then Dorian's whispered "Water" in her mind caused her to stare at the river beyond her enemy. Ships and boats were realizing that trouble was at hand and moving out of the way, but she couldn't devote too much concern to them. They would have to fend for themselves. Her foe would have the whole city in flames if she didn't deal with him, and knocking him into the water seemed like the most logical choice.

She instructed, "Quentin, keep shooting at him. I'll try to put him in the water."

Onyx had landed cleanly and immediately unslung her bow, drawn a lightning arrow, and launched it at Fire Guy. She snarled a curse as her arrow met the fire shield and disintegrated like the bullets the others were firing at it. The lightning had flashed but did nothing useful. The fire arrows in her quiver would do no good, so she was left with the third option, the explosive-tipped arrows.

When she'd tested one, it had destroyed the target, leaving her a little daunted at the arrow's destructive power. A further worry was the danger of carrying such explosives around on her back. They required magic to prime, but she could see a situation where she was hit in the back by an attack and they somehow exploded anyway, killing her. As a result, she only carried two.

She drew one out and aimed it at the fire guy's head as she pulled back the string. She released it and it flew true, but out of nowhere, another enemy entered the fight by blasting her arrow out of the sky from the ground with a forked bolt of lightning.

Onyx fired three fire arrows at him as he flew toward her, releasing them as quickly as she could. The first one went wide, and the electric man blasted the other two away before they reached him. He landed ten feet away on the balcony and shot lightning at her from both palms as if telling her to stop.

She dropped the bow, dove forward in a shoulder roll

to avoid the barrage, and pulled her clubs from her belt. They were already full-size, so she was able to use them to attack immediately as she came up to her feet. They struck his lightning shield, and the sizzle made her hair stand on end. She laughed at the feeling. "Maybe I should see you before my next night out."

Onyx had thought of him as a creature, but now that she was up close, she could see he had once been an elf. His features were distorted, though, swollen and lumpy. He looked like he was in pain, and she vowed inwardly that if she could figure out how to help him when this was all over, she would.

The thought fled from her mind as she leapt to the railing to avoid one blast of lightning, then did a backflip back down to the balcony to dodge the next. "If anyone's free, I think I need some help with this guy."

Quentin replied, "Sorry, Onyx, I don't have an angle." He fired another bullet at the fire guy, only to see it vanish before impact again. He wished he had specialized ammunition. Hell, he wished he had a howitzer at this point.

A whisper of instinct at the back of his mind caused him to roll sharply to his right. The veil fell from an enemy hovering over the rooftop nearby, beyond the anti-magic field. Quentin's brain wondered how he could do that, but then he was too busy rolling in the opposite direction to avoid the next force blast the new arrival sent at him.

The anti-magic field was sure to offer some protection, but he wasn't sure how high it reached and didn't dare trust his life to it. He got to his knees, lifted the sniper rifle, and shot from the hip. The bullet struck the force creature and spun him around, but when he turned back to face Quentin, the only change was that his twisted visage was now full of rage. "I need a little help up here, people."

Billie snapped, "Shadow, help Cueball. Stretch, give Onyx a hand if you can." She yelled, "Jilly, the roof," and saw the dragon, who had been darting in to attack Fire Guy every time he turned away from her, change her trajectory.

Billie readied herself. "Here goes nothing. Dorian, any help you can give me would be appreciated."

The dagger replied in her mind, *Channel all your power through me.* She wondered if he could handle that much, and the dagger laughed as if he'd heard the thought. *I have worked with beings far more powerful than you, wielder.*

She hissed, "Rude," under her breath, then stopped throwing attacks at Fire Guy and began building up her magic. Bullets continued to hit him from CIR, her team, and the Spellbound people. She had no idea what was going on in the big picture anymore. The fight had come down to her versus Fire Guy, and the combat tunnel vision she was usually able to avoid took complete hold of her.

When she had all the power she could contain built up, she sent it through Dorian with a scream. Its passage was visible in how the air shook as the magic moved through it, expanding out into a cone from Dorian's tip, which she had stabbed at the creature. The wave of magic struck, and Fire Guy flew backward as she had intended. Hope surged, then impossibly, he didn't fall but flew backward to land cleanly on a barge full of shipping containers.

Billie snarled, and Quentin interjected, "Yeah, Basher, that's who I need help with. Flying force dude. But thanks for distracting him for a minute, anyway."

"Well, hell, then there's only one thing for it." She ran forward, gathering speed and building up her power, then blasted force magic into the ground at the edge of the street. She flew into the air, headed for the container ship, ready to sink it if that was required to take out Fire Guy.

Anya had been firing at the lightning guy, sneaking bullets in when Onyx was far enough away that there was no chance the pixie would get into the line of fire, when Billie told her to help Quentin. She'd blasted force magic into the ground to send herself flying up toward the roof of the convention center but had only made it to the second floor on the first effort. A second one brought her to the roof, where her magic vanished an instant before her boots hit the gravelly surface.

Quentin had deployed his bulletproof shield and was using it to protect himself from the force blasts as they came down, occasionally firing at the attacker with his pistol. As she got close, he advised, "The anti-magic shield weakens the attacks. I'm not sure he can hurt me through it, but I don't really want to find out."

Anya gave the command to deploy her shield and drew her pistol. Even if their foe couldn't hurt them through the anti-magic field, they needed to take him down before he caused any more trouble for their teammates. She and Quentin fired steadily at him, and finally a bullet got through and red blood blossomed. But not enough, and a moment later, a piece of HVAC equipment from a nearby building flew at them, forcing them to hastily reposition.

Hannah warned over their comms, "Incoming. Shadow, keep him distracted."

Anya collapsed her shield and used her rifle to fire one shot after another. Quentin did the same with his pistol, and together, they kept the enemy's attention on them. Hannah flew into view from the side with her shotgun braced against her shoulder and pulled the trigger when she was only six feet from the force wielder. The slug slammed into his torso and caused him to tumble out of sight.

Hannah landed awkwardly on the roof and slid a distance before she got control of herself. Quentin and Anya ran to the edge of the building and saw their attacker on the ground below. As he stood, Anya used her rifle to pour bullets into him while Quentin fired rounds from his sniper rifle. Caleb added his shotgun to the barrage at ground level.

It took thirty seconds, but finally their adversary stopped moving. There was no time to rest. Lightning Guy and Fire Guy were still up, and Anya was sure the longer they stayed that way, the worse it would be for her team and this city.

CHAPTER THIRTY-ONE

Billie had landed cleanly on top of a triple stack of cargo containers. She had wrapped herself in fire and ice, then added additional force shields atop it. It was rare for her to devote so much power to defense, but she figured that if she couldn't defeat him, keeping him occupied would increase their overall chance of winning. She wished again that she had a frost grenade and made a mental note to ask Eileen if that was possible.

She threw magic at the creature, but even her frost only struck his flames and vanished. He was ridiculously strong, and she couldn't understand how he was able to sustain it. She growled, "Not fair that he should be this powerful and have such a large magic reservoir."

Quentin replied, "Shadow and Bomber are on their way over to help. Just hold on."

Distracted for an instant by the comment, Billie failed to note the fire whip that snapped out, wrapped around the shields at her ankles, and yanked her feet out from under her. She landed on the containers with a clang that echoed off the other boats, but her shields protected her from injury. They continued to do so as Fire Guy dragged her down to a two-stack, then down to a single stack.

She coated Dorian in frost and slashed through the line before he could bring her all the way to the boat's deck. She vaulted to her feet and saw him forming a giant fireball. "Uh-oh."

Jilly zipped past her ear. The little dragon flew at the fireball, then tucked herself into a ball at the last second. She passed through the fireball and apparently through the creature's shields, because he staggered backward as if he'd been punched. The fireball dissipated unused. Jilly hurtled out of the flames, then uncurled and launched into the air.

Billie called, "Shadow, Bomber, I need you to do something."

Anya replied, "We're free."

Billie threw frost attacks at Fire Guy and jumped from container to container to avoid his counterattacks. "I need a wave. However you can make it. Crash it down over this boat. Pull in any other magicals who are around to help. As big as you can."

Hannah warned, "I'm not sure we can control it once it's up. Might knock some containers off."

"That's fine."

"Might knock you off."

Billie snorted as she ducked under a fire lance that blacked the nearest container. "I can swim."

Shadow replied, "You got it. Thirty seconds."

Onyx had so far avoided most of the lightning attacks her foe had thrown at her, although one had burned along her neck and up her cheek intensely enough to make her tear up. She'd tried using her clubs but had been unable to penetrate his shields with them. After several more inconclusive passes, she dashed down the balcony, grabbed her bow, jumped to the railing, and leapt off.

She turned in midair, drew her last explosive arrow, and fired it at the surface between her foe's feet. She landed cleanly at street level and rolled to absorb the impact. When she came up, Lightning Guy was on street level as well, looking dazed as he stumbled toward her.

Onyx pulled arrows from her quiver one after the next, not caring what kind she got. Fire arrows, lightning arrows, and regular arrows hit his shields and failed to make it through the electrical defenses. She had begun to feel like he was impossible to beat when he suddenly staggered forward like someone had punched him in the back of the head and fell. Caleb stood behind him with his shotgun's barrel smoking.

Onyx looked at her teammate. "I had him, you know."

He aimed his shotgun down and fired into the man's legs as he tried to rise. "Sure looked like it, what with all the flailing around."

"You're not a nice man."

He chuckled. "Not the first time I've heard that. Now, help me keep an eye on this trash."

Billie had changed position as she attacked Fire Guy, moving him around so his back faced the shore that housed the convention center. He sensed the danger at the last moment and spun as the wave crashed down over them.

Billie had anchored her feet to the deck with force bands and gripped more of them in her hands as she fought against the momentum of the wave crashing against her shield. When it was gone, Fire Guy was drenched, his flames finally extinguished. She felt a moment of triumph before steam rose from his body, which she took as a signal that he was working to restore the fire.

Jilly flashed in from the side in Billie's peripheral vision and passed behind the creature. He bellowed something like a scream and fell backward, indicating the dragon had done something damaging to his legs. Billie ran forward with Dorian extended and blasted frost magic out of it in a continuous stream to cover Fire Guy as if he was unintentionally on fire and she was the extinguisher.

For a moment, she thought she had him fully encased. Then flames broke out to shatter the shell she'd built around him. She drew her pistol and shot him once in the leg, surprised when the bullet made it through. She lifted the barrel to point at his chest. "Maybe we can help you if you don't make me kill you."

He didn't respond, but the temperature increased dramatically, signaling that he was doing something.

Izzy warned, "Boss, he might be explosive."

"Dammit." Billie looked around at all the boats that would be destroyed if there was an explosion, then pulled the trigger until the gun was empty and Fire Guy was motionless. She holstered the pistol and turned in a slow circle to assess the damage he had caused. Behind her, the river was aflame. She frowned at the unexpected sight. "Why is the river on fire?"

Danica's voice was full of mirth and laughter as she replied, "It does that historically, apparently. Welcome to Cleveland."

It took them several hours to wrap things up at the site. All three elemental attackers had been killed, and the local FBI had dispatched a unit to transport the bodies to a lab for research purposes. After showers and changing into normal clothes, everyone had gathered at a local bar to wind down after the mission. Only four of them remained as Thursday turned to Friday. Onyx and Jilly were holding down a nearby table together, and Danica and Billie were seated at the bar. The former had an IPA in hand, and the latter sipped a cosmopolitan.

Danica had received a call a few minutes before, and as she disconnected and tossed her phone on the bar, she released a heavy sigh. "While the assault at the convention center was underway, another group attacked the company, both the server and the headquarters campus. The main research building was significantly damaged and might have to be imploded. They can't tell if anything was taken because it's all wrecked inside."

"Were any of your people there?"

Danica shook her head. "No, thankfully. Our gig is to

watch over the CEO. Which I'm guessing just got a touch harder."

Billie stirred her drink with a swizzle stick. "What kind of damage?"

Danica took a long pull of her beer. "Elemental."

"What a coincidence."

The other woman laughed. "Right?"

Billie signaled for another round and drank her glass dry. "Maybe the bodies from the convention center attack will point back to Genovary."

"Yeah. And maybe we'll all win the lottery tomorrow." Danica laughed darkly. "That's probably more likely, really."

"Well, for sure, Genovary has just become a focus of the Magical Threats division of the FBI."

Danica's head bobbed. "Appropriate. Good luck with that."

Billie slid a twenty-dollar bill across to the bartender as their drinks arrived. "Thanks. I think we're all going to need as much luck as we can get."

<hr>

Derik Cote sat in his office with his feet up on the desk. Outside the large windows that dominated one wall, he could see the DC city skyline. Nearer, a holographic image of a man materialized in the center of the room. Derik stood and approached the image. "Did we get what we wanted?"

"Yes, sir."

"And Genovary?"

"Believes they are the only ones who received the data, as agreed."

Derik nodded. That was one of several promises he'd never intended to keep. "We inserted the flaw?"

"As planned. The infomancers say it went off perfectly."

He grunted. "I'll believe it when I see it. But good. The facility in Oregon?"

The other man had stood at attention during the questions, but now a small smile crept in at the corner of his mouth. "Has the data and is beginning a full review."

Derik smiled in return. "Well done, Spencer."

"Thank you, sir."

Derik shrugged on his jacket, then tugged his cuffs out from underneath them. "I'm off. That hot DJ is playing at Club Barrage again tonight."

Spencer laughed. "Maybe I'll join you then."

"Do. I'll buy you a drink or three. You can help me charm her."

"See you there."

THE STORY CONTINUES

The story continues in book three, *THREAT LEVEL: LIGHTNING,* coming soon to Amazon.

AUTHOR NOTES: TR CAMERON

AUGUST 12, 2025

Thank you so much for reading the second book in the FBI: Magical Threats Division series! If you've read Spellbound Secruity, I hope you enjoyed seeing some familiar friends. If you'd like to grab the free prequel story, *Threat Level: Unknown*, you can find it here: https://BookHip.com/PJWZPFW

The elemental enemy theme will continue, although it won't be the only foes Billie, Onyx, and the others will face. Book 3 will deepen the intrigue of the corporation genetically modifying magicals and engage more directly with the main villain.

I realized in this book that I've got way too many characters with names that start with "E." Ethan, Elaine, Eileen, Erin. Apparently my brain was locked in a rut when I came up with the names this time around.

Book 1 is coming out tomorrow as I'm writing this, and

as recently as yesterday we were still tweaking things. One of the Just-in-time reviewers is a Veteran who suggested that my weapons choice for the team was problematic. By the time it's out, it will be fixed. When an expert tells me a thing, I defer.

I'm on a plane to Houston, TX right now. My kid is in the window seat beside me. We have a series of running jokes, one of which we're really only able to use at the airport, John Mulaney's routine about Delta airlines. Its still funny.

I've said this before, but I think this might be my last Oriceran series for a while. I love the Universe, but I don't have a clear inspiration for where to go next. It might be time to build out my own world and play in it for a while before returning to this one when an idea blossoms. Time will tell. I have six more of these to finish (yay!) before I can start a new thing anyway.

I like Onyx. Book 3 will have her making good on at least one of her sparring challenges. The bow and pixie dust both have potential for new and entertaining iterations. And her attitude is great.

I've dropped hints about Billie needing to color outside the lines. That will move forward in book 3 as well. Writing in a series that's understood to be a series from the outset offers the opportunity to seed things from one book to another, which I like. I know that it can often feel like a loose end, though, and I hope the speed of the releases helps with that.

In that vein, I have to talk about *Penny Dreadful*. It's on Paramount +, and has an absolutely amazing cast. Eva Green, Timothy Dalton, Josh Hartnett, Billie Piper, and a range of smaller roles that are nonetheless brilliant. It ended as it had to, given the way the story worked, but the ending failed to close the stories of *most* of the characters, which felt unusual and awkward. A good storytelling lesson, really.

I need to find the discipline to generate words on this trip. I have the tools with me. It's just a question of making myself do it. I've backed myself into a corner (again, this is a thing that I do again and again like I'm addicted to the angst it causes) and can't afford not to. Hopefully that will help me break whatever it was that has stopped me in the past.

We saw Anthony Greene a third time. It was the best of the three. Truly a magical show, at a great venue in Baltimore called Ottobar. Saw Ke$ha at Blossom, where we hid out from the rain and heat in the overpriced but very timely purchased Green Room. Next shows are Enhypen and Ateez, both K-pop boy bands.

When we get back, we have 3 days at home before we head to Toronto for My Chemical Romance. The kid got sick and we missed the first MCR show we had tickets for. So we're going to the Chicago show to make up for it at the end of the month. Next month is so full of stuff it's already fallen out of my head. I just know we're really busy and Lady Gaga is in there somewhere and we might go to Denver to see Anthony Greene a ridiculous fourth time.

The kid and I saw *Superman* and *Fantastic Four* in the theatre. Those two plus *Thunderbolts** are the most heartfelt superhero movies in an age. I really liked all of them. Superman we saw twice. James Gunn has us. We'll see all the DC releases until something disappoints. Although I didn't like *Peacemaker* season 1. I might have to try again. We also watched *Now You See Me*, a heist movie with magicians and I'm so happy to say the kid liked it. This opens up the heist movie vault, and I have so many that I love. Plus we can watch the sequels to NYSM together for the first time.

Star Wars *Acolyte* was good. I'm glad I watched it. And I'm watching *Star Trek: Strange New Worlds* Season 3 in real time at the moment. It's been really good so far. I love the cast. I'm hoping that some of the good ideas that are bouncing around for Trek come to fruition. Having seen the previews for *Starfleet Academy*, I'm a little concerned about that one, not going to lie.

Doctor Who went away from our streaming service and doesn't have a home at the moment. It's weird not to be watching it. Still working our way ever so slowly through *Daredevil Reborn*. I've started watching pieces of *Westworld* again, but that won't stick. I need to watch

Sandman season 2 and *The Last of Us* season 2, but I'm not in the right mental space for either at the moment.

Still listening to Robin Hobb's tales of Fitz and the Fool. Finally at the third book, about 33% through. I love her storytelling style, but this trilogy is so different than the others that it's hitting me weird. Great story as always though. I'm also relistening to John Scalzi's Interdependency trilogy, which is great snarky fun.

I have so many video games I want to play and no time to do it with. But I'll choose adventures with my kid over video games any time.

I hope you'll join me for book three of FBI: MTD! Until then,
joys upon joys to you.

One of the Best Conversations I Ever Had Was at a Gas Station

It was the kind of place you pull into when your tank is low and your brain is somewhere else. A small, dusty station just off a long Texas highway. The kind where the lights hum, the chips are a little stale, and the clerk might be both the cashier and the mechanic if you ask nicely.

I wasn't expecting a conversation. I wasn't expecting anything at all, honestly. I just needed fuel—both the literal kind and maybe a little more than that.

I was in the middle of a stretch of my life that felt... blank. You know the kind. You've gotten through the hardest part—maybe the divorce, the diagnosis, the move, the loss—and now you're just trying to figure out what comes next. No map. No applause. Just a dusty road and a pit stop.

And then this woman, probably late sixties, standing in front of me in line with a floral tote bag and one eyebrow raised like she'd seen too much, turned around and said, "You look like you've been somewhere."

Not *you look tired* or *what's wrong.* Just that:

"You look like you've been somewhere."

I blinked. "I guess I have."

She nodded like she knew what I meant.

That started a five-minute exchange about places we'd been, both the kind you can find on a map and the kind you carry in your heart. We talked about living alone, how silence can be both comfort and punishment. She told me she'd been widowed twice. I told her I'd survived cancer five times. We didn't flinch.

No small talk. No pretending.

She said, "Sometimes the hard parts sand off what doesn't matter. You're just left with the truth. That's the good part."

And then she bought a Mountain Dew and walked out like she hadn't just dropped wisdom like a lightning bolt in the snack aisle.

I never saw her again. I don't know her name. But I've never forgotten that conversation.

Here's the thing:

We spend so much time trying to plan the big moments.

But it's the unexpected ones that crack us open.

It's not always the mountaintop epiphany or the perfectly timed breakthrough. Sometimes, it's someone in line behind you who reminds you you've survived. And maybe even changed for the better.

That's something I write into my stories again and again.

In *The Peabrain Adventures*, Maggie finds wisdom in the

weirdest places—people others dismiss, places she almost overlooks. In *Hellhound Academy*, Robin keeps running into strangers who carry keys to her past. Avery, in *The Last Sanctum*, often stumbles into insight while she's looking for something else entirely.

These characters, like me, are learning to stay open. Not just to magic, but to humanity. To chance encounters. To conversations that don't look like anything special—until they are.

I used to be someone who powered through. I didn't leave room for interruption. I thought progress came from planning and pushing. I had no time for gas station prophets or quiet chats with strangers.

But now?

Now I leave space.

Now I listen.

Now I believe some of the best things in life happen when you least expect them.

Maybe that's the magic: not that someone gives you the answer, but that someone sees you. Even for a minute.

That woman at the gas station didn't know me. But she saw something. And in seeing me, she reminded me that I wasn't invisible. That my journey—twists, scars, and all—was visible to someone else.

That's powerful. And free. And available to all of us.

I think we all have a story like that tucked away. A moment we didn't expect that changed something in us.

And maybe the next one is still ahead.

Maybe it'll happen at a coffee shop or in the checkout line or right when we think nothing's coming.

Maybe it'll be *you* who says something that shifts the sky for someone else.

And maybe that's the best kind of adventure. The unplanned kind. The quiet kind.

Like a five-minute miracle in a dusty gas station when you thought you were just getting a fill-up. More Adventures to Follow.

OTHER SERIES FROM T.R. CAMERON

Urban Fantasy

(with Martha Carr and Michael Anderle)

FBI Magical Threats Division (8 book series)
Federal Agents of Magic (8 book series)
Magic City Chronicles (8 book series)
Rogue Agents of Magic (8 book series)
Scions of Magic (8 book series)
Secret Agent Witch (8 book series)
Spellbound Security (8 book series)
The Nomad Witch (8 book series)
Witch Warrior (12 book series)

Science Fiction

(with Martha Carr and Michael Anderle)

Azophi Academy (4 book series)

CONNECT WITH THE AUTHORS

TR Cameron Social

Website: www.trcameron.com

Facebook: https://www.facebook.com/
AuthorTRCameron

Martha Carr Social

Website: http://www.marthacarr.com

Facebook: https://www.facebook.com/groups/
MarthaCarrFans/

Michael Anderle Social

Website: http://lmbpn.com

Email List: https://michael.beehiiv.com/

https://www.facebook.com/LMBPNPublishing

https://twitter.com/MichaelAnderle

https://www.instagram.com/lmbpn_publishing/

https://www.bookbub.com/authors/michael-anderle

BOOKS BY MICHAEL ANDERLE

Sign up for the LMBPN email list to be notified of new releases and special deals!

https://lmbpn.com/email/

For a complete list of books by Michael Anderle, please visit:

www.lmbpn.com/ma-books/